A Far Country

G.T. DUNN

A Black Horse Western

ROBERT HALE · LONDON

First published in Great Britain 2001

ISBN 0 7090 7007 1

Robert Hale Limited
Clerkenwell House
Clerkenwell Green
London EC1R 0HT

Typeset by
Derek Doyle & Associates, Liverpool.
Printed and bound in Great Britain by
Antony Rowe Limited, Wiltshire

1

Curtis McKenzie eased his palomino pony to a halt atop the ridge and surveyed the tricky descent which lay before him. In the valley far below, the tightly-packed adobe buildings basked peacefully in the bright orange glow of the fiery late-spring sunset. A thin carpet of slushy snow still covered the steeply winding trail that led down to the old Spanish settlement of Santa Fe. The clear skies overhead coupled with the rapidly falling temperature held the promise of an overnight frost. With a weary sigh he instinctively pulled his heavy buffalo-skin coat tighter about his neck in response to a chilly gust of wind before setting off down the slope, trusting in the sure footedness of his mount to see him safely off the mountain.

It was fully dark when he entered the almost deserted, muddy streets of the town an hour later. Both his horse and trailing mule found the going tough as they plodded their way through the quagmire on main street *en route* to the Santa Anna

Cantina, where McKenzie intended getting warm on the outside and wet on the inside.

When he strode in through the swinging doors, he found the *cantina* to be populated by a handful of locals, drinking, jawing and playing poker. The great caravans of freight wagons which rolled in from Kansas at regular intervals throughout the summer and autumn months, bringing supplies to the expanding frontier, turning the settlement into a thriving centre of commerce and disturbing the peace, would not make an appearance for several weeks yet. The mule-skinners and freighters who earned their living on the Santa Fe trail were a tough, uncouth, hard-drinking, hard-playing breed who knew how to handle themselves with fist, knife and gun. They hated Indians with a passion, due to the frequent lightning raids on the caravans, and regarded any sign of weakness in a man as a mortal sin. Only the fiercely independent mountain man was regarded as an equal – and McKenzie was just such an *hombre*.

McKenzie made his way to the bar where he ordered a whiskey, which he paid for with a silver dollar. 'Leave the bottle,' he instructed as the Mexican bartender filled his glass.

'It is early for you to be down from the mountains, *Señor*,' observed his host, replacing the cork in the bottle.

'Aha,' replied McKenzie non-committally, downing the fiery liquid in one long swallow, instantly coughing in response to the burning sensation in his throat.

'What'd you brew this from, snake venom?'

'No, my friend,' said the grinning bartender over his shoulder as he turned to polish a stack of dusty glasses on the rear shelf, 'that's genuine rye whiskey all the way from Kentucky.'

'Could have fooled me!' exclaimed McKenzie.

'You have furs to trade?' The mountain man nodded. 'Juan Martinez, that's him playing cards over at the table yonder, the one wearing the sombrero, he will give you a good price for your merchandise,' advised the Mexican, nodding towards the man in question.

'Did you say Juan Martinez?' queried McKenzie. His genial host nodded.

'Do I know you?' queried a voice from the table on hearing his name spoken.

'We ain't ever met,' replied McKenzie, taking the whiskey bottle and his glass from off the counter as he started across the dirt floor in the direction of the card players. 'But you wrote me a letter late last summer, about a package you were holding from my wife back in Boston.'

'You certainly took your time getting here,' remarked the Mexican trader, throwing in his hand. 'I fold, Ricardo. The cards are not being kind to me tonight.'

'The trapper you sent word with didn't find me until the first snows came to the high country,' advised McKenzie, pulling up a chair at the table in response to the Mexican's gesturing hand, 'so I figured it would keep until spring. Though I can't for the life of me figure out why you didn't just send it up and save me the trip.' Martinez and his three companions looked at each other and laughed. 'Do you mind tellin' what's so gall-danged funny?'

'We mean no offence, *Señor*,' insisted Martinez. 'It's just that your package is not the usual kind and your delay has cost me much money.'

'How can a parcel cost money to look after?'

'I think you should accompany me to my house, then you can see for yourself,' advised Martinez, rising from his seat. 'Come, it is not far.'

Although he felt dog-tired and wanted nothing more than to finish his bottle and then get a good night's sleep, McKenzie was intrigued by both the Mexican's behaviour and what the package contained, so he followed him out through the swinging doors of the *cantina*. He hadn't seen or heard from his wife in the thirteen and a half years since he'd headed west to seek his fortune. For his part, he had written to her only twice in all that time, just to let her know he was still alive and to inform her that if she ever needed to contact him, she could send word to him via Santa Fe, where he came to trade most summers.

In truth, his heart had never been set on marriage. It was something his well-meaning, deeply conservative, parents had forced upon him in the hope of settling him down and putting an end to all his foolish notions about a life on the western frontier. Not that he had ever found Anna-Marie, the only daughter of gritty, Irish immigrants, to be a disagreeable gal – far from it. She was pretty, high-spirited, intelligent, witty and not afraid of hard work. For two years they had lived quite happily and made the best of things on their smallholding to the south of the sprawling city of Boston. But the problem was, Curtis McKenzie was not cut out to be a farmer.

From as far back as he could remember, he had been gripped by a wanderlust, an all-consuming passion to visit the great American wilderness, to experience at first hand the things he had read and heard about. He hankered after a fresh start, far from the eastern settlements that he found so interminably dull and the petty local politics that smothered ambition. Unfortunately his wife did not share his dreams and made it perfectly clear from the outset that she wanted nothing more from life than a farm that would provide them with a steady income to support a house full of kids. She loved their land with its meandering stream, fertile soil, wooded hillsides and simple two-roomed log cabin built from the sweat of their own labours. She had no wish to abandon it for an uncertain future in a far-away territory populated by savage Indians and wild animals.

No matter how hard he tried, there was simply no changing her mind. Then came that fateful day in 1849 when he heard of the gold strike at Sutter's Mill in California. McKenzie knew he had to try his luck at striking it rich in the newly-discovered goldfields.

He asked Anne-Marie to go with him, but she steadfastly refused. They argued about it for several days, her fiery Irish temper leading to many a cooking pot flying through the air in his direction. When it became obvious that nothing she could say would change his mind, she reluctantly gave her blessing, promising to join him in California once she had found a buyer for the farm.

He headed west with a small grub stake a week later, but nothing went according to plan: he never reached California and she never left the farm to join him. It was something she never did get around to explaining to him in any of her letters, even though she had a good reason for staying put.

'We'll get your horse and mule stabled first, my friend,' said Juan Martinez as the two stepped out into the muddy street. 'The folks here in Santa Fe are an honest lot, by and large, but a pile of winter furs will fetch a good price, so it is best not to put temptation in their path. Then I'll take you to my home so you can view your package.'

Mission accomplished, they squelched their way through the deep, clinging mud to the friendly Mexican's single-storey adobe home at the far end of town. Having wiped the mud from their boots, the two men stepped inside, where they were greeted by Martinez's charming and very attractive young wife, Juanita. She quickly poured them glasses of wine, then lifted an oil lamp from a table in the corner and led the way into the kitchen, where she insisted that their guest was fed before whatever business the men had was attended to. McKenzie didn't argue, for he was extremely hungry, and certainly ready for a pleasant change from his own trail cooking.

The mountain man found his host to be most agreeable company. They chatted away like old friends while Juanita fussed over them like an old mother hen. The chicken stew and seasoned dumplings she served up certainly hit the right spot. McKenzie couldn't remember when he had last eaten so well, and he said as much. Juanita giggled and pretended to feel embarrassed as she cleared the solid oak table at the end of the meal. Martinez refilled his guest's glass from the vintage bottle of Spanish wine his wife had selected from his vast cellar.

'You certainly have a taste for the finer things in life, my friend,' offered McKenzie.

'I work hard, and I have always believed that a man should enjoy the fruit of his labours,' replied his genial host, resting back in his tall chair. 'Do you not agree?'

'Sure,' said McKenzie, affably, 'but fine wine and fancy furnishings are somewhat hard to come by up in the mountains.'

'It is a lonely lifestyle you have chosen,' sighed Martinez, offering his guest a cigar from the box his wife had just handed him. 'But one day, civilization will come to the wilderness, then everything will change.'

'That's what I'm afraid of,' said the trapper, nodding his thanks as the Mexican lit his cigar, 'change and people crowding in. I like my life just the way it is. Oh it's hard at times, I'll grant you that, but I'm free to live it the way I please. So you might say, I'm a contented man, Señor Martinez.'

'I'm glad to hear it.'

'Now what about this package of mine that you're holding?'

'Let us enjoy our smoke first,' insisted Martinez, 'there is plenty of time, my friend.' When they had finally finished their cigars, the Mexican picked up the oil lamp from the table and led McKenzie down a narrow passageway to a small curtained-off room at the back of the house, When Martinez drew back the curtain, McKenzie saw that the room contained a bed, and beneath the covers, just beginning to stir, was a young girl. She sat up rubbing her eyes.

'What do you want, Señor Martinez?' she asked, softly. 'Who is that man with you?'

'Do not be frightened, little one,' said Martinez, smiling reassuringly, 'it's only your papa. He's finally come to collect you.'

The look on the mountain man's face was a picture to behold. 'What is this, Martinez?' he demanded, gruffly. 'I ain't got no daughter.'

'Oh, but you do, Señor,' insisted the merchant. 'I have a letter for you in the bureau in the main room. It will explain everything. Come, we will fetch it, for we must allow your little girl to sleep. You can leave her here until the morning.'

The Mexican took hold of his bemused guest by the arm, shepherding him gently back into the main part of the house. In the makeshift bedroom a rather nervous thirteen-year-old girl wasn't at all sure she liked the look of the man the kind Señor Martinez said was her long-lost father. Somehow, he wasn't at all what she had been expecting!

2

Little Josie McKenzie was small for her age, but what she lacked in physique, she more than made up for in spirit and pure dogged stubbornness. She was normally a happy, extrovert, mischievous character, who possessed a wicked sense of humour as well as her deceased mother's sharp Irish tongue and quick temper. However, her pa's cold indifference towards her coupled with the strangeness of her wild surroundings, had for once awed her into silence.

They hadn't exchanged more than a few words since he had come for her at first light. She could tell by his demeanour that he was far from pleased to be saddled with a daughter he hadn't even known existed, and she felt exactly the same way about the tall, bearded, rough-looking man who was not exactly the handsome, dashing figure of her dreams, or ma's obviously romanticized description.

Hour upon hour they climbed ever higher into the rugged, beautiful mountains, via the narrow, slippery precipitous trail, with only the soughing of the wind through the tall redolent pines and the eerie cries of the hawks in the clear blue skies overhead to disturb the stoic silence between them; As she rode the pack mule in step behind her pa, she mulled over all the important questions she had wanted to ask on meeting him, but was now too nervous to voice. Eventually, curiosity and frustration finally got the better of her.

'Where are we going?' When he chose to ignore her, she repeated her question, making no effort to mask her irritation. His stubborn silence caused her to lose her cool. 'Why are you ignoring me?' she demanded, brusquely.

'Hold your tongue, gal, and let me concentrate on the road ahead,' he replied

Angry words quickly formed in her throat, but she wisely decided to leave them unspoken. Gritting her teeth, she took her frustration out on the mule, kicking it none-too-gently in the flanks. The shocked animal bellowed with rage and bucked for all it was worth, depositing her hatless, bruised and wet in the middle of the slushy trail.

'What the heck are you doing?' demanded her pa over his shoulder, reining in his mount.

'The dumb critter threw me,' she complained, climbing painfully back to her feet, brushing herself off. 'My pants are all wet, I'm all uncomfortable. I'll have to change into my spare pair.'

'On no you won't!' replied McKenzie. 'You'll get back in the saddle and ride jest the way you are. It might teach you to treat your mount with a mite more respect.'

'Respect!' exclaimed a pouting Josie, climbing to her feet. 'What about showing me a little more respect?'

'Less of your sass, my gal,' warned McKenzie, 'or you'll be walking on account of your rump being too sore to ride. Now move it, pronto.'

With an exasperated, 'Uuuh!' and having poked out her tongue, but not until his back was fully turned, Josie slowly and reluctantly obeyed.

The wind became keener the closer they drew to the high pass between the jagged peaks that towered before them. The ominous grey clouds gathering in the north and the bitterly cold air held the promise of a dusting of snow before the day was out. Feeling decidedly cold, damp and miserable, Josie sensibly gave the mule its head as it picked its way carefully up the trail. The unhappy child was totally oblivious to the spectacular scenery all about her. Her thoughts strayed back to her former home on the farm and the loving mother and grandparents who had all succumbed in turn to the virulent smallpox epidemic which had ravished the country all around Boston almost exactly a year earlier. It had been her mother's dying wish that Josie should head west in search of the father she had never known. Now she was almost wishing she had died too.

The bright sun was high in the sky when McKenzie reined in and announced that it was time to eat and rest their mounts. Having unsaddled and tethered the animals within reach of fresh grass, McKenzie withdrew some strips of beef jerky from the mule's pack and held them out to his daughter.

'What's this?' she queried, putting the visually unappealing food to her nose.

'Something to keep the hunger from your belly,' he advised, plunging his hand back inside the pack to feed himself.

'It smells like old leather,' she observed, prior to taking a bite. 'Tastes like it too.'

'Well, it's all you're gettin' until we make camp fer the night, so make the most of it,' he insisted, squatting down on a rock. Biting off a large piece of the jerky, he began to chew on it contentedly.

'Ain't ya gonna boil us up some coffee to get rid of the taste of this stuff?' she asked.

'No time,' he replied. 'We've still got a long ways to go before nightfall, so you'll have to make do with water from the stream over yonder.' He rose from his seat and craned his neck to check on the weather. 'Snow's coming,' he offered, prior to wandering off to relieve himself in the trees. 'Be sure to fill your canteen before we set off.'

'He treats his horse a damn sight better than me,' she muttered under her breath, as she slowly and grudgingly rose from the ground to do his bidding.

Father and daughter did not exchange another word throughout the entire afternoon as they made steady progress through the long, wooded valley in the shadow of the towering, jagged peaks which seemed to reach up to the very heavens. The trees afforded them some welcome protection from the gathering wind. Dark clouds duly arrived to block out the sun and, just as McKenzie had predicted, by late afternoon it began to snow quite heavily. The relentless icy flakes stung their exposed faces, forcing them to seek shelter, which they ultimately found in a small cave close to fresh water. McKenzie soon had a fire going.

'Get that inside of ya,' he said, handing a cup of steaming black coffee to his half-frozen daughter. 'That'll soon get the blood flowing through your veins again.'

Josie rubbed her numb hands together vigorously before accepting the proffered cup. She carefully sipped the scalding hot, slightly bitter tasting coffee, savouring the warm sensation it soon generated in her hungry belly. 'When do we eat?' she asked, cradling the cup in her tingling finger. 'I'm starving.'

'Just as soon as we've taken care of our mounts,' he replied, pouring himself another cup of coffee. 'They need a rub down and some fresh oats.'

'Can't we do that after we've eaten?'

McKenze shook his head. 'The animals always come first,' he insisted. 'By rights we should have seen to their needs before we even lit the fire. Look out for your mount and it'll look out for you. You'd do well to remember that, city gal.'

She glared at him angrily, but held her tongue. When her pa rose from his seat on the far side of the comforting fire and moved away to see to the welfare of the animals, she took the hint and hurried after him to lend a hand.

'Watch yourself, the ground's a mite slippery underfoot,' he warned on hearing her fall into step behind him.

'Ya don't say!' she exclaimed, making no effort to slow her pace. Almost immediately she felt her feet slip from under her. She crashed to the ground, arms and legs all akimbo, her head just missing a large round boulder at the side of the clearing.

'It might pay you to listen in future,' he said without breaking stride or so much as a backward glance, 'if'n ya want to survive in these here mountains.'

Josie clambered slowly and painfully back to her feet, eyes blazing with anger, unable to comprehend why he was being so insensitive. His conduct was both hurtful and puzzling. With a shake of her head, she set off after him through the swirling snow.

Almost her entire life she had longed to meet the pa who had headed west before she was born. Many a night she had lain awake for ages in her room trying to imagine what he looked like, the kind of person he was and how it would be to share his exotic lifestyle. Her impressionable young mind had conjured up visions of a tall, rugged, handsome, daring frontiersman who could wrestle bears with his bare hands and kill Indians by the dozen when the need arose, but who was kind and gentle towards women and children. Boy, had she got it all wrong! While there was little doubt he was tough, in all other respects he was a bitter disappointment to her.

Having taken care of their mounts, they wasted no time in returning to the comparative warmth of the shallow cave. McKenzie put some fresh wood on the fire then casually threw a bright red blanket in the direction of his dispirited child.

'Get some shut-eye,' he said, as she caught hold of the blanket in her right hand. 'We leave at first light.'

With a brusque nod, she spread the blanket out on the rock hard ground close to the fire and settled down for the night. By eastern standards she was a pretty tough kid who had always accepted her lickings without fear or complaint. Tears did not come easy to the proud, stubbornly independent youngster; indeed apart from the day when her ma died, she could not remember the last time she had cried. But now silent tears came all too easily as she lay listening to the howling wind, waiting for sleep to claim her.

3

It was still dark when McKenzie shook his sleeping daughter firmly by the shoulder, bringing her awake. Throwing back her blanket, she sat up with a yawn, blearily rubbing sleep from her eyes. When her pa disappeared outside to check on the animals and the state of the weather, she climbed stiffly to her feet, then wandered off in search of a suitable spot to relieve herself. The snow-covered ground was still hazardous underfoot, so she took great care not to repeat her mistake of the night before. Although the air felt cold and crisp, the stars shone brightly in the pre-dawn sky, indicating that the storm had long since passed.

McKenzie had a fire going by the time she returned to the cave. 'There's some beef jerky left if you're hungry,' he said, handing her a cup of coffee. She shook her head.

'I'll just make do with coffee.'

'Suit ourself,' he replied, refilling his own battered

cup from the enamel pot before dousing the fire with the remaining liquid. 'Drink up, it's time to ride.'

Daybreak brought a change in the direction of the wind and a considerable improvement in the weather. Clear blue skies and a gentle breeze held the promise of a perfect late-spring day in the high country. By mid-morning the bright sun was beginning to melt the overnight snow. It felt pleasantly warm on their backs as they continued on their upward trek into the wooded high country. Eventually, McKenzie became so hot that he was forced to remove his thick, sturdy, buffalo coat. He laid it across the front of his saddle and then reached for the canteen at his hip. Having taken a long sip of cool water, he glanced back over his shoulder and said, 'Want some?'

They were the first words he had spoken since setting out. His daughter merely shook her head as she gazed towards the dense forest which stretched for as far as the eye could see along both sides of the valley. The natural beauty of the tall pines, rugged peaks and babbling brook were in stark contrast to her increasingly black mood. Her ma's death had been a terribly hard thing to bear at such a tender age, but the prospect of building a new life in a far country with her father had helped to ease the pain and her sense of loss. In the long, intervening months in between, she had managed to convince herself that freedom and excitement lay before her, but after just one full day in his company all her illusions had been well and truly shattered. Now she was beginning to wonder if she wouldn't have been better off living in an orphanage in Boston rather than with a such a cold, unfeeling stranger.

The eerie cry of an eagle winging its way through the azure skies high above brought her out of her trance. Shielding her eyes against the dazzlingly-bright sun, she inclined her head skywards to follow the bird's graceful journey back to its nest in the rocks at the northern end of the valley. When she felt the animal between her knees come to an unexpected halt, she instinctively kicked it in the flanks, oblivious to the fact that the animal had responded to her pa reining in ahead of her. It was only when the baying mule collided with her pa's stationary filly that she realized her mistake.

'What in tarnation do you think you're doin'?' he demanded, whirling about to face her.

'I'm sorry,' she said, all flustered, 'I wasn't paying attention.'

He was all set to give vent to his anger when he heard the drumming of horses' hoofs emanating from the depths of the forest. A split second later a dozen riders burst into view on the far bank of the stream.

'Indians!' exclaimed a frightened Josie, giving the mule another kick.

McKenzie swiftly grabbed hold of the animal's bridle to prevent it from taking off back down the trail. 'Just keep still and try not to act scared,' he said, turning back to face the approaching Indians.

'But I am scared!' she insisted.

'There's no need to be,' he said, calmly. 'They're Utes, and Utes have always been friendly towards whites.'

'They don't look very friendly to me,' she observed, her heart beating more rapidly with each passing second. As the Indians drew closer she couldn't help but notice the menacing bright red and black paint daubed on their stern, bronzed faces. Although she knew very little about the savages who inhabited the untamed frontier, she was pretty darned certain she could recognize a wad party when she saw one.

The Utes quickly forded the shallow stream and reined in directly in front of McKenzie and his skittish daughter. Their leader, a tall, muscular, bronzed figure who wore a single eagle feather in his shiny black hair, raised a hand in greeting and nodded towards the mountain man.

'Hello, Wanaka,' said McKenzie, in Ute. 'It's good to see you, my friend.' The warrior grunted.

'You are far from your cabin, McKenzie.'

'I had to take a trip into Santa Fe to fetch my daughter home.' The Indian instantly looked puzzled.

'I didn't know you had a daughter. You have never spoken of her.'

'I didn't know about her either until I got to Santa Fe,' replied the mountain man. He quickly explained the circumstances which had brought Josie west.

'She is scrawny and ugly,' observed the warrior, giving her the once-over.

'She's more than that,' offered McKenzie, 'she's a right pain in the ass.'

Although Wanaka maintained a deadpan expression, several of the other warriors laughed at the trapper's observation. A young buck, who McKenzie judged to be no more than sixteen, nudged his pony forward at the walk for a closer inspection of the little girl. He circled around, finally halting directly in front of her mule. Although she didn't understand what they were saying, Josie surmised, from the laughter and the youth's behaviour, that she was the topic of conversation.

'What are you gawking at, you ugly son-of-a-bitch?' she hissed, safe in the knowledge that he wouldn't understand what she had said.

She got the shock of her young life when the scowling boy replied in broken, heavily-accented English, 'A stupid, puny white girl!' The young warrior turned to face McKenzie. 'You want sell girl?' he asked, in the language of his own people. 'I think she make good wife after I beat some manners into her. For her I give you my best pony and two good blankets.'

McKenzie chuckled, then shook his head. 'I won't say I ain't tempted,' he chortled, 'but it ain't our custom to let a gal marry so young. Come back in a few years and we'll talk about it.' The youth grunted.

'Young Bear think you make big mistake, McKenzie,' he said. 'Girl cause you much trouble. You should let me take now to train properly.'

'I'm truly grateful for your generous offer, Young

Bear, but like I say, it's not our way,' insisted the trapper, all smiles.

'If girl like father, Young Bear should be grateful McKenzie say no,' interjected Wanaka. 'She may look small and weak but me think you would be taking on more girl than you could handle.' His observation caused great merriment amongst the assembled warriors as well as embarrassment to Young Bear.

'I reckon you're right about that,' agreed McKenzie, ruffling his mount's ear. 'But while it's been good chewing the fat with my ole friend Wanaka, I've still got a long ride ahead of me this day, so if'n you'll excuse me, I'll be on my way.'

Wanaka leant forward to lay a restraining hand on the reins of McKenzie's horse. 'There is much trouble in the mountains this spring,' he said, locking eyes with his friend.

'What's happened?' queried the mountain man, raising his eyebrows.

'There was a raid on one of our villages three nights ago.'

'Shoshones?'

Wanaka shook his head. 'The raiders rode shod horses and were white. They took horses, furs and scalps.'

'Scalps?'

The warrior nodded. 'They must be caught and punished.'

'I agree,' said McKenzie. 'But why would whites attack your people? There has never been trouble between us. The Utes have always been friendly towards all the mountain men, it just don't make any sense.'

'No,' agreed Wanaka. 'It is a very bad thing. These cowards killed women and children. Now many at our council fires talk of driving all whites from our mountains, that none can be trusted. I think war will come unless we find them quickly.'

'Such talk makes my heart sad,' sighed McKenzie.

'You have nothing to fear,' insisted Wanaka. 'You are one of us. We know where your heart lies. But there may soon come a time when all others who live in our mountains will pay for the foolishness of those who attack peaceful villages.'

'Your anger is understandable,' said McKenzie. 'But it is wrong to direct it against those who have never done you harm. There must be a dozen or more trappers like me who come to these mountains every year who would never do anything to hurt your people.'

'I know this,' replied Wanaka. 'I spoke out against war and offered to find those who murdered my people, which is why I am here now. But the trail has gone cold. The snow has covered their tracks and I fear that if we return empty-handed to our camp the hotheads who talk of war may get their way.'

'Your father is wise,' said McKenzie, 'he would not allow this.'

'Yes, Grey Bull has the wisdom of an owl,' agreed Wanaka, 'but as he grows old and his eyes dim, so does his influence at the council fire. Other voices now shout him down.'

'Then I can only hope that you find them before it is too late,' offered the mountain man. 'I wish you good hunting, my friend.'

Wanaka shook hands in whiteman fashion with McKenzie. He then wheeled his mount about and led the war party away at the trot. When they had finally vanished from sight, a deeply concerned McKenzie set off towards the head of the valley, beckoning to his frightened daughter to follow.

'What did they want?' she asked nervously, from the rear.

'Oh, they jest stopped by to say howdy,' he lied, staring straight ahead. 'Though the youngster you insulted had a hankerin' to take you for his bride.'

'I'm surprised you didn't give your permission,' she said, irritably.

'I told him he should come back for you in a couple of years,' he replied, happily. His words immediately had the desired effect, for she fell silent and remained that way throughout the rest of the day. It enabled him to focus his attention on how best to help all his friends in the mountains, red and white, avoid a bloody conflict. By the time they made camp for the night he knew exactly what he had to do.

4

Late in the afternoon of their fifth day in the high country they entered a small, secluded valley where the grass grew tall, spring flowers bloomed in a myriad of majestic colours and the sunlight danced upon the sparkling clear waters of a shallow stream alive with trout. Pine trees grew on the precipitous mountain sides, although not as tall or as thickly as those they had encountered in the dark forests. They paused briefly to water their mounts and take in the grandeur of their surroundings before riding on. When Josie craned her neck to peer towards a building in the distance, her pa simply said, 'Home.'

The sound of their approach brought curious, smiling faces to the doorway of the single-storey log cabin that had been built right up against the sheer, rocky cliff at the western end of the valley. 'Do they live with you, too?' asked Josie on catching sight of the pretty young Indian woman and young boy who came out to greet them.

'They are my wife and son,' advised McKenzie.

'But ma was your wife!' exclaimed his shocked daughter.

'Was is right.'

'How could you betray mom like that?' she demanded incredulously, hardly able to believe what she was hearing.

'I don't reckon I have to justify myself to you,' he said, 'but for your information, the mountains can be a mighty lonely place for a man, especially in winter when you can be snowed in for months on end.'

'But there's a law against having two wives!'

'Not as far as the Utes are concerned,' argued her pa. 'And besides, I knew I'd never see your ma again, she never had any intention of heading west to join me. From the first moment I set eyes on Star I knew she was everything a man could ever want in a wife. Ain't she jest the most beautiful girl you've ever seen in your life?'

'No!' snapped Josie rather rudely, on reaching the cabin.

Star was in her husband's arms almost before his feet touched the ground. They embraced warmly as their young son came to join them. The youngster hugged his father warmly and then quickly asked him, in the language of his mother's people, about the girl who was still sitting quietly astride the mule. McKenzie's explanation brought a frown to his face. However, Star immediately accepted the situation for what it was, promising her husband that she would be a good mother to his daughter. Their son glared up at his new sister and made some pointed remark which caused them to laugh.

'What's wrong with him?' demanded Josie tetchily, pushing her sombrero further back on to her head.

'Little Hawk thinks your hat would look better on the mule, and you know what, I reckon he's right!' tittered her pa.

'Oh, yeah, that's real funny,' she sneered, slipping gracefully off the animal's back. 'At least I don't dress like some filthy Indian brat!'

In the blinking of an eye, Little Hawk had let go of his pa's arm and was halfway towards his truculent half-sister, intent on teaching her some manners. McKenzie managed to grab hold of his lithe, irate eleven-year-old son by the sleeve of his buckskin jacket in the nick of time. 'Quit it!' he ordered, in English, as the boy continued to struggle to reach his new sibling. 'And you hush your mouth, too,' he added, glaring at Josie. 'Little Hawk's your brother, and you are going to have to learn to get along, so be nice.'

'He ain't no kin to me,' she hissed, defiantly.

'He's of my blood, and that makes him your brother,' insisted her pa, his face clearly showing displeasure at her remarks.

Little Hawk ceased struggling, turned to face his pa and said in perfect English, 'Why did you bring her here?'

'Like I said, she had nowhere else to go,' replied McKenzie, maintaining a tight grip on the youngster.

'You can't choose your relatives,' he added with a wry grin, in an attempt to inject some levity into the situation, 'you jest have to make allowances fer them and learn how to live with them.'

'I'd rather scalp this one!' insisted the boy, reverting back to the Ute language. 'But then again, I'd probably blunt my best hunting knife on her thick head.' The mischief that fairly sparkled in his dark eyes indicated that his temper was beginning to cool. McKenzie let go of his son's sleeve and patted him affectionately on the shoulder.

'If she had other relatives to look out for her, I would not have brought her here,' he said. 'My daughter has an acid tongue and a fiery temper, just like her mother. She is not used to the ways of the mountain, so we must give her time to adjust. I will need your help to keep her safe. I'm relying on you.'

'I would rather try to tame a cougar,' said Little Hawk, 'but I will do as you ask.'

'Good,' replied his pa, tousling the boy's long, shiny, jet-black hair. 'Now how about rustling us up some rabbits for supper?' The youngster nodded, then made off towards the cabin to collect his hunting bow. 'Let's get you settled, Josie.'

When a coyly smiling Star moved to assist her with her things, Josie pointedly placed her own body between her new mother and the mud-caked mule. 'I can manage,' she insisted.

'As you wish,' said Star, wishing to avoid creating a scene.

Irritation flared in her husband's face, but she quickly put a finger to her lips to still the rebuke she knew was coming. She understood the little girl's reticence in accepting the presence of a new woman in her life. Josie had lost her own mother and was now about to live amongst strangers. It would take time for her to come to terms with the situation and accept the love and protection of a new family. She also knew her husband all too well, and was certain that he would not have displayed any obvious warmth or concern towards her during their long and arduous journey. His apparent indifference would have left her feeling confused and hurt.

While Curtis McKenzie was truly a loving husband and devoted father, he was also a very private man who often found it difficult to show his true feelings. He did not court friendship amongst his fellow trappers, though he called no man his enemy. He had won the universal respect of his peers and the Indians with whom he shared the land. They recognized him for what he was: a devout, scrupulously honest, decent sort of man who possessed a keen sense of fair play. Although he tended to keep his own company, he never turned his back on any man in trouble or one who sought his advice.

Like all mountain men, he was tough, stubborn, independent, resourceful and fiercely proud. It was the only way a man could survive in the harsh, unforgiving world of the Rocky Mountains. But there was another side to his character, known only to his wife and son: that of a warm-hearted family man who cherished the rich beauty of the remote yet fulfilling life he had chosen for himself and his loved ones far from the crowded, so-called civilized towns of the east. And knowing how difficult it was to reach this inner-self, she harboured no doubts that the shock of finding himself with a daughter to support would have meant he would have kept her at arm's length right from their first meeting up until the moment they arrived at the cabin in the sheltered valley.

She also knew it would take time and patience for them all to make the necessary adjustments in their lives. Patience was a commodity Star possessed in abundance, just like the ancient prophet named Job, whom her husband sometimes spoke of during the long dark winter nights, when he read from the battered old leather-bound copy of the Christian Bible he kept in the cabin. There would be difficult times ahead for all of them, but things would work out.

Josie slowly, and somewhat reluctantly, followed her pa and Star into the gloomy cabin. 'You'll have to sleep on the floor next to Little Hawk for tonight,' said McKenzie, as his daughter stood motionless in the middle of the floor surveying the slightly cramped, musty quarters of her new home through disappointed eyes. It was not at all what she had been expecting, being nowhere near as spacious, comfortable or exotic as the pictures she had conjured up in her mind. 'I'll fix you up a mattress tomorrow, when I've had a chance to cut some of that tall grass down by the rock pool.'

'Fine,' she said with a resigned sigh, throwing her belongings down on the floor by her half-brother's bed, 'but don't put yourself out on my account.'

Over supper McKenzie broke the news of the unprovoked attack on the Ute village and his encounter with Star's brother, Wanaka. His wife listened in silence, her brown face expressionless, as he spoke of his concern for the safety of the other mountain men who roamed the high country and what war might mean to both sides.

'You have nothing to fear,' she assured him. 'I do not think my father would allow our young warriors to attack the trappers who are known to us.'

'I'm not so sure,' insisted McKenzie. 'Like Wanaka said, your father grows old. The warriors may not choose to listen to his wise counsel.'

'Even so, we will be safe whatever happens. There is not one among the Utes who does not regard you as a brother.' He merely nodded as she took his empty bowl and crossed the dirt floor to the stove to refill it with steaming hot meat and wild vegetables. 'What will you do?' she asked upon her return.

He shrugged his shoulders. 'I think I might take a ride over to your father's camp in the morning to talk things over with him. Maybe I can dissuade any of the young hotheads from causing trouble.'

'I think I have seen the men who raided the

village.' Little Hawk's quietly spoken announcement took them all by surprise.

'Where? When?' queried his father, staring into the youngster's dancing eyes. 'And what makes you think it was them?'

'I was out hunting late in the afternoon three days ago,' said Little Hawk. 'I saw them riding west towards Turkey Creek.'

'What makes you think they are the ones?'

'Although I didn't think about it at the time, it is very unusual for so many mountain men to travel together in spring. They rode in close formation, like a war party.'

'Did they spot you?'

Little Hawk smiled. 'Do you think I travel through the forest like a noisy white man? No, of course they did not see me.'

'How many were there?' His son informed him there had been six riders. 'And if they were heading west then it means Wanaka's band are looking in the wrong place.'

'Perhaps we should go track them for my uncle,' suggested Little Hawk. 'I would enjoy the challenge of a different kind of hunting, one with scalps on offer!'

'You're stayin' home,' stated his pa firmly, having paused just long enough to swallow another mouthful of the delicious belly-warming stew. 'This ain't gonna be no picnic.'

'But you need me,' argued the excited youngster. 'I

know where to pick up their trail, and anyway you can't handle six of them alone.'

'The answer's no,' insisted McKenzie.

'It ain't fair!' snapped Little Hawk petulantly, folding his arms across his chest. 'If it weren't for me you wouldn't know anything about them or where to look, and now you're planning to up and leave me behind while you have all the fun.'

'The one thing it won't be is fun,' corrected his pa in response to his son's not unexpected tantrum. 'These are callous, cold-blooded killers who wouldn't think twice about gunning down anyone who gets in their way, including a rambunctious kid still wet behind the ears who has more sass than sense.'

'That's telling him!' interjected Josie. It was her one and only sulky contribution to the supper-time conversation. She sensed rather than saw the kick that came winging her way from the pouting boy on her right and just managed to nimbly draw her leg out of harm's reach before he could enact his revenge.

'Quit it, both of you,' warned their pa, feeling the table move. 'Clear the dishes and go wash up.'

'I'm a guest,' replied Josie. 'I shouldn't have to do chores.'

'Even guests have to pay their way in the mountains,' he growled. 'Now get moving, gal, before I take a strap to your rear end.' When she shot up out of her chair, defiance blazing in her green eyes, he thought he might have to go through with his threat, but his pointed finger and warning, 'Git!' finally did the trick.

With an irritated, 'Humph,' she grabbed hold of an armful of dirty dishes and marched off in a huff towards the sink.

'Finish clearing the table then go fetch a pail of water from the stream to do the dishes, Little Hawk,' instructed McKenzie.

'You sure it ain't too dangerous for me to go wandering around outside in the dark?' queried his son, provocatively, as he set off to do his pa's bidding.

'Jest keep it up and you'll be in line for a leathering too!' promised McKenzie.

'He is his father's son,' interjected Star as the boy closed the cabin door behind him.

'Ain't no doubt about it,' he agreed, grinning broadly. 'But he don't yet know his limitations. You'll need to keep an eye on that little varmint when I leave in the morning. I wouldn't put it past him to go sneaking off after me the first chance he gets.'

'I will watch him like the hawk he is named after,' promised Star.

As soon as the children had finished washing and drying the dishes they were sent straight to bed. Josie didn't utter one word of complaint, as she wanted to maintain the illusion that her long ride had left her completely exhausted. Star supplied her with a makeshift pillow and a couple of warm, brightly coloured blankets, which she spread out on the floor next to her half-brother's bed. The adults then retired to their curtained-off room at the far end of the cabin happy in the knowledge that the new addition to their family was sleeping peacefully.

5

Sometime during the night McKenzie heard the door of the cabin creak open. Figuring it was merely one of the children stepping outside to answer an urgent call of nature, he turned over and went back to sleep. The next thing he knew, Star was shaking him by the shoulder.

'What's up?' he asked. When she informed him that Josie was missing he said, 'She must have jest stepped outside for a moment.'

Star shook her head as he sat on the edge of the bed and reached for his pants. 'The mule is gone, too. I think she has run away.'

'Hogwash,' he argued. 'Where would she go?' Star shrugged her shoulders.

'Back to Santa Fe, maybe? I am afraid she will find only danger in the mountains. You must find her, and quickly before any harm befalls her.'

'I'll find her all right,' he promised, coming to his

feet and buckling on his gun-belt, 'and when I do, she won't sit down fer a week.'

Little Hawk was eating breakfast at the table.

'Why didn't you stop her?' asked McKenzie, moving towards the door.

'I didn't know she was set on leaving,' replied his son, defensively.

'If anything's happened to her, you and I will be having words, boy,' promised his pa.

'It ain't my fault she ran off,' argued Little Hawk, 'it's yours. I heard her crying and complaining to herself all last night. Seems like she don't reckon you want her around.'

'That's preposterous!' exclaimed McKenzie. 'We ain't rightly had a chance to get to know each other yet, so how can she go jumping to such darned-fooled conclusions?'

'That's girls for you,' offered his son, impishly.

McKenzie experienced no difficulty in picking up her trail. The mule tracks retraced the route they had taken to enter the valley the previous day. He judged that she had a good two hours head start. With a good horse beneath him and a sound knowledge of the country, he figured he could overtake her before nightfall, if she was truly of a mind to ride all the way back to Santa Fe . . . sooner if her real purpose was simply to make a point. As it turned out, he caught up with her a good deal sooner than he expected, and it was lucky for her that he did.

Around noon one set of tracks became two: those of

the mule and a young child afoot in hostile country. It brought a satisfied grin to his face, for it could only mean one thing: her cantankerous mount had somehow managed to get away from her. He pushed on down the trail happy in the knowledge that he was now likely to find her more quickly.

The nerve-shredding call of a hungry cougar stalking its prey carried to him on the light breeze as he made his way south through wooded country. He knew Josie had to be its intended prey. Reaching for the trusty old Hawkins rifle he carried in his saddle-boot, he urged his mount forward at the canter. As he rounded a bend in the muddy trail, he saw his terrified daughter cowering on the ground with her back pressed up against a large boulder. The crouching, hissing, cat was all set to close in for the kill. While a cougar will seldom risk attacking a fully-grown, healthy adult, a child was viewed as easy pickings. However, the angry report of a rifle shot echoing through the mountains as it pinged off the rocks inches above its head caused the snarling cat to take flight into the forest without so much as a backward glance.

McKenzie dismounted with a scowl and a shake of his head. He glared down at his trembling daughter and said, 'What in God's name did you think you were at, running off like that? If I'd gotten here a minute later you'd have been feeding that cougar's young fer a week!'

'You mean you actually care about what happens to

me?' she demanded, sarcastically.

'What the heck are you sayin'?' he demanded, yanking her roughly to her feet by the sleeve of her jacket. 'Of course I care. You're my daughter ain't ya?'

'Yeah, I'm your daughter, but you sure ain't been acting like you was really my pa.'

'I ain't ever heard such nonsense,' he snorted. 'Why I've a good mind to haul you over my knee and tan you good for being so sassy, not to mention all the trouble you've caused me, young lady.'

'Go right ahead,' she cried, throwing her sombrero petulantly to the ground in front of her, 'I've been spanked before.'

'Why you ornery, little filly,' he said. Maintaining his tight grip on her arm, he squatted down on a fallen tree trunk and hauled her over his knee. 'You've really got this coming.'

'Why don't you like me?' Her unexpected question caused him to hesitate with his hand poised to strike. With a sigh, he swung her up to sit astride his knee.

'What makes you say such a thing?'

'The way you've been acting,' she observed, wiping away her tears. 'Ever since we first met you've either been scolding me or ignoring me.'

'This isn't like Boston, Josie,' he said. 'It's a harsh land where one mistake can be your last. A mountain man needs to stay alert and quiet on the trail, but I can see how you might misinterpret my silence as indifference, and I'll also admit that the idea of having a daughter has taken some getting used to.'

'So I was right, you really don't want me around?'

'I never said any such thing,' he insisted, indignantly. 'And anyway, if that were true, why did I come after you?'

'I don't know,' she sighed. 'Maybe you felt duty bound.'

'You are one stubborn kid, you're jest like—'

'My mother,' she said, cutting him off in mid-sentence. He nodded. 'Why did you run out on her?' Her unexpected question caused old wounds to resurface.

'Is that what she told you?' he demanded, irritably. 'That I ran out on her?'

'No,' she replied. 'She never talked about you, so I had to figure things out for myself.'

'Well you figured wrong,' he insisted. 'But this is neither the time nor the place to talk of such things. We need to be getting home.' He slid her gently off his knee as he came to his feet. 'Star will be worried about you.'

'Why would she be worried about me?' demanded Josie. 'She hates me, and so does that son of yours.'

'Now don't go sayin' that,' he said. 'It was Star who sent me out after you, and, like me, Little Hawk just needs some time to get to know you. He's a good kid, Josie and I feel sure you two are gonna become great pals. In fact, he kinda reminds me of you.'

'In what way?'

'Well, you're both feisty and full of devilment, and like you he'll always fight his corner and take his licks when he's in the wrong. He also has your quick temper, too.' He guided her gently towards his waiting mount. Having swung up into the saddle, he offered her his outstretched hand and effortlessly pulled her up behind him.

'Are we going after the mule?' she asked, wrapping her arms around his midriff.

'No,' he replied, wheeling about. 'There's no point. The chances are that ole critter's already providing a meal for the wolves or the Utes.'

'And it's all my fault. I wish I could pay you for him.'

'Oh, don't worry, you will,' he assured her. 'I'm gonna work your tail off all summer till I figure you've cleared your debt.'

6

Little Hawk's mood was as black as the storm clouds hovering over the mountains to the north as he answered his mother's call for a bucket of water from the stream. He knew that Josie's foolhardy stunt was likely to cost his pa any chance of catching up with the evil men who had raided the Ute camp. The coming rain would wash away any sign that had survived the snow of the day before. He was angry with her for deflecting their pa from such an important task, but he was also mad with himself for allowing it to happen. He could easily have raised the alarm when he heard her leave the cabin during the night. Sheer spite had caused him to hold his tongue. He didn't like his cantankerous new sibling one little bit and was glad to be rid of her. Yet he also felt guilty, for he knew he had acted badly and possibly made his pa ashamed of him. His pig-headed foolishness was also likely to lead to the renegade trappers getting away with their cowardly raid on the Ute camp.

His mother was hard at work in the kitchen, curing the skins of the two rabbits her young son had killed for supper the previous evening, when he entered the cabin. She smiled at him and indicated with a nod of her head that he should place the bucket on the floor by her feet. 'My son grows strong,' she stated. 'There was a time when he would have needed to drag such a load, now he carries it with just one hand.'

'We need fresh meat for supper,' he said casually, as an idea suddenly popped into his head. 'Pa may not return before nightfall, I think maybe I should go hunting.'

She looked up from her labours at the kitchen table just long enough to shake her head and say, 'Your father said that you were to stay home until he returned.'

'But we have to eat,' he insisted, knowing she was going to take some persuading, 'and by the time pa gets back he'll be too tired to hunt. I won't go far, and I'll be real careful.'

She gazed deeply into his pleading eyes and then, against her better judgement, she gave up the fight. 'Stay within the valley and return by noon, rain is coming.' He was out of the door, bow in hand, knife in belt, like a shot, before she had a chance to reconsider.

Having saddled his black pony, he made off across the stream towards the far end of the valley, cutting a wide loop, just in case his mother was watching. When they were well clear of the cabin, he turned his trusty steed south-east in the direction of Turkey Creek.

It took him the best part of an hour to reach his objective. The melting snows higher up the mountain had turned the normally tranquil creek into a raging torrent of foaming, frothy water. He dismounted and tethered his pony within easy reach of grass and water before wandering off to look for sign. His keen eyes soon homed in on the clear impressions of a number of shod horses in the soft ground. He quickly collected his mount and set off in pursuit, just as rain began to fall from the leaden sky.

For the best part of an hour he carefully followed the tracks of the riders, but as the rain became harder, his task grew more difficult. Eventually all sign of the riders vanished in the muddy morass before him. A seasoned tracker might have done better, but not a cold, wet and inexperienced child who was rapidly coming to terms with the fact that he was out of his depth. Sitting astride his pony, atop the rocky ridge where the trail had finally gone cold, feeling throughly dispirited, he shivered in response to the fierce wind blowing directly into his exposed face and the icy water dripping from the brim of his hat on to his already saturated clothing. The mountain peaks on either side of him were hidden by the low-lying banks of dark cloud, a clear indication that the rain had probably set in for the day.

His head told him it was time to give it up as a bad job and head home with his tail between his legs. He knew he'd get a licking from his pa for his foolishness, but that didn't weigh half as heavily on his tender shoulders as his sense of failure. A whipping, for daring to make a mistake, he could accept with a good grace as he had before – it was a natural part of growing up; but defeat was much harder to bear, which was why he let his heart rule his head. Although he knew full well he had one chance in a thousand of locating his quarry, and every prospect of catching pneumonia, he stubbornly eased his mount down the slope.

The ground was steep and slippery underfoot. One careless mistake would have sent them tumbling out of control on to the jagged rocks far below. When he paused by the swollen stream to get his bearings, his mount snorted and started to prance about impatiently. 'Quit that!' he ordered, pulling back on the reins. When the animal failed to respond, he surrendered to its wish to keep moving by turning upstream towards the mouth of the red-rocked canyon.

The youngster lost all track of time in his desperate and forlorn attempt to pick up the trail again. It was only when the rain finally eased to a steady drizzle that he realized he had come too far to return home by nightfall. He was going to be in a lot of trouble. When he reined in halfway across a high grassy plateau to ponder his predicament, he suddenly detected a hint of wood-smoke hanging in the damp air. He stood tall in the saddle and gazed towards the range of low-rolling, pine-covered hills that lay dead ahead. Although there was no smoke to be seen, he knew that someone had made camp within the protection of the wooded hillsides.

Whoever it was, they were used to the ways of the mountains, for they had not used green, smoke-producing branches to build their fire. They had acted wisely and done all they could to mask their presence, but good fortune had smiled on Little Hawk. He had stumbled across those he sought at the very moment that he was about to admit defeat.

Although merely a boy, he was well-schooled in the art of moving quietly and unobserved through the wilderness. He just needed to hold his nerve and remember all he had been taught. It was vitally important that he didn't let the excitement of the moment overtake him, for one momentary lapse in concentration might cost him his life. He cautiously edged his pony forward at the walk through the ankle-high grass, keeping all his senses alert for any possible sign of danger.

The smell of burning wood became even more pronounced when he drew abreast of the nearest hill. He slipped silently out of the saddle and led his pony into the shelter of the trees, where he picketed him safely beside a tall pine. His heart was racing uncontrollably as he placed his bow and quiver of arrows over his right shoulder and paused to consider his options.

He was playing a highly dangerous game, for the men he was up against were hardened killers who wouldn't hesitate to add a child to their list of victims, should he fall into their clutches. Up until that moment he hadn't stopped to think about what he would actually do if and when he pinpointed their camp. With the element of surprise working in his favour, coupled with his skill with a bow, he might be able to kill one or more of the renegades, but he wasn't naïve enough to figure he could handle the whole bunch without help.

His best chance of success lay in trying to run off their horses. Once afoot they would be sitting ducks when his pa or the Utes finally caught up with them. His skill and daring might also persuade his pa to ignore his blatant act of defiance. Having taken a deep breath to calm his nerves, he stealthily made his way through the tightly-grouped pines in search of his unsuspecting enemy.

Within a matter of minutes he was crouching low behind a large bush atop a gentle rise some fifty feet from their fire, taking stock of the situation. The raiders had chosen an excellent spot for their camp, right beside a small waterhole in a sheltered gully less than two hundred yards from where he had left his pony. A pot of coffee simmered over the fire, while round about their wet clothing lay spread out to dry over saddles and packs. In his cold, wet and uncomfortable state he was envious of the comparative warmth they were enjoying. Right then he would have given just about anything for a hot meal and a fresh set of clothes.

The men's horses and pack mules were tethered amongst the gently swaying trees at the far end of the gully. In order to reach the animals undetected, he would have to circumnavigate his way around the camp and approach them downwind, from the rear. Although his pa had carefully nurtured his hunting and survival skills from an early age, he knew that sneaking into an armed camp would be the ultimate test of his abilities and courage.

His plan was far from foolproof. Many things could go wrong: a bird suddenly taking flight; a twig snapping beneath a careless foot; or one the animals catching his scent on the breeze would instantly betray his presence. They would then have little problem in running him to ground before he could make it back to his waiting pony. He was scared, but having come so far, he knew he had to see it through. A fierce determination burned deep within him. He would make his pa proud of him. Little Hawk was about to become a warrior.

He didn't make his move until twilight settled upon the land and the woods were cloaked in darkness. Through the gathering gloom he could just make out two shadowy shapes deep in conversation, silhouetted by the light of the fire. Their relaxed, imposing manner caused him to hesitate momentarily. Serious doubts returned to haunt him as he swallowed hard in a vain attempt to still his rapidly beating heart. The men below somehow seemed even taller, broader and more menacing than he had anticipated. Could he really risk pitting his skills against those of a band of seasoned mountain men and cold-blooded killers? His fearless young Indian cousins, who took great pride in their ability to steal horses right from under the noses of their Shoshone enemies, would view it as a simple challenge, but he was only half-Ute!

It took him fifteen patient minutes to reach his objective undetected. He surveyed the apparently still and silent campsite from behind a bush. There was no sign of the two men, so he assumed they had turned in for the night. Everything was working like a charm, and although the trickiest part still lay tantalizingly before him, the element of surprise appeared to be working in his favour.

Success would ultimately depend upon speed of foot, keeping a cool head and a fair slice of luck. Once in the open, he would have only a matter of seconds to cut loose and stampede their mounts before making good his escape.

He rose from his kneeling position and, keeping low to the ground, sprinted across the narrow clearing in the direction of the picketed animals. No sooner had his knife cut the first horse free than a muscular arm clamped itself tightly around his upper torso from behind, knocking his hat off and pulling his arms to his side. He instinctively kicked and fought for all he was worth in a vain attempt to break free, but the man was far too strong for him. When he felt the point of a knife prick the skin at his throat he instantly ceased struggling.

'Drop your knife,' ordered his captor gruffly, keeping his own blade close to the boy's throat. When Hawk complied, the man loosened his grip on his heaving chest and then swiftly retrieved the discarded knife, which he placed in his own belt. 'Pick up your hat and then walk towards the fire, slow and easy. And no tricks or you'll get this knife stuck up between your ribs.' Hawk wisely chose to comply.

A second man was waiting for them by the fire. 'What in tarnation do we have here, Jed?' he queried, incredulously. 'Is this pint-sized little runt the critter who's been blundering around our camp for the past hour?'

'Yeah,' advised his companion, spinning Hawk about to face him. 'Now I have but two questions for ya youngun', and you'd better answer straight up, if'n you know what's good for you. Who are ya? And why were you tryin' to steal our horses?'

Little Hawk stared sullenly at the ground between his feet. He didn't want to tell them anything, even though he felt deathly afraid. Jed viewed his captive's stubborn silence as insolence rather than fear, so he cuffed him hard across the side of the head to encourage him to loosen his tongue.

'If I have to ask again, boy, I'll use my knife on you, then you'll talk fer sure, you can count on that,' he sneered. The terrified youngster never doubted for a moment that he was the sort of man who was quite prepared to carry out such a threat.

'My name's Little Hawk, Little Hawk McKenzie.'

'Not Curtis McKenzie's boy?' interjected the other trapper from the far side of the fire. Little Hawk nodded. 'Is your pa with you?' The boy shook his head. 'Well I'll be dog-goned. Now what the heck are you doing way up here all on your lonesome?'

'I was tracking you.'

'What do you mean, you was trackin' us?' demanded the one called Jed. 'We ain't been anywhere near your place.'

'I know what you did, my pa told me about the Utes you raided.'

'What in tarnation are you talkin' about, kid? We ain't laid eyes on a Ute since last Fall.'

'You're a liar, mister!' insisted the boy, defiantly.

'I don't take kindly to some young whippersnapper calling my word into question.'

'I don't care, I'll say what I like. You're gonna kill me anyway, just like those innocent women and kids you scalped. But my pa won't let you get away with it, nor will the Utes. They'll find you now fer sure. My tracks will lead them right to you.' The man locked startled eyes with his partner across the fire.

'What do you make of this crazy kid, Joe?' His companion merely shrugged his broad shoulders as he pulled his blanket tighter about himself.

'You say someone attacked a Ute village?' he asked.

'Yeah, you!'

' 'Twern't us, boy,' he insisted, solemnly shaking his head. 'No sir, I'll swear it on the Holy Bible, Joe and me had nothin' whatsoever to do with it.'

'We're tellin' the truth, kid,' interjected his partner, adopting a friendlier tone of voice. 'We've been wintering up in Shoshone country, only arrived in these parts yesterday.'

'Why should I believe you?'

'You say the killers took scalps?' asked Jed. The youngster nodded. 'Well go check our packs. I guarantee you won't find no Indian hair.'

'Maybe your other friends have the scalps,' argued Little Hawk.

'What other friends? Joe's the only pal I got. Him and me are partners, we work alone.'

'I've only got your word for that.'

'God, but you are one stubborn kid!' exclaimed Jed. 'What do we have to do or say to convince you that we're telling the truth?'

Little Hawk was beginning to suspect they were who they said they were. But he wanted to be absolutely sure before giving them his trust. He thought things over for a moment and then said, with a deadpan expression on his dirty, tired face, 'Well, for a start, you could give me my knife back.'

'If we do, the little savage'll probably slit our throats,' mused Joe, sitting down astride a log by the blazing, crackling fire. 'Though by the sound of things, he'll merely be saving the Utes the trouble.'

Jed withdrew the youngster's knife from his thick, leather belt and handed it to him, handle first.

'Are you hungry, young fella?' asked Joe, figuring,

correctly, that he hadn't eaten all day. When the boy nodded, the trapper rose from his seat to see to his needs as their guest sheaved his knife.

'I'd say you're also a mite cold and wet, judging by the way you're shakin' all over there, little pard,' observed Jed, laying a friendly arm on the boy's trembling shoulder.

'Here,' said Joe, offering him a bowl of the rich venison stew from the pot which was gently simmering over the fire, 'get that inside ya and you'll soon feel better.'

'First get those wet clothes off,' interjected his partner, handing him a blanket from his own bedroll. 'Wrap this around you while we dry your duds off by the fire overnight.'

It took the shivering youngster a good few minutes to fight his way out of his wet clothing, due to the fact that it stuck so uncomfortably to his damp skin. After completely disrobing, he wrapped the rough blanket around his naked body before squatting down on the ground in front of the fire to eat his stew.

Having eaten his fill, Little Hawk settled down to sleep by the fire, safe in the knowledge that come daybreak, his hosts planned to reunite him with his pa. He knew his pa would be scouring the mountains for him, and that he would be big trouble when he got home, but at that particular moment he was too tired to care.

7

The smell of fresh coffee on the fire and the chirping of the birds in the woods brought Hawk awake as dawn broke in the eastern sky. He arose with a yawn to reclaim his dry clothing. A night spent on the hard earth had left him feeling like an old man. Mind you, he suspected that he'd be a good deal sorer once his pa got hold of him!

After breakfast he helped his new friends load their furs and provisions on to the backs of their pack animals. 'You don't have to take me home,' he said, as they prepared to set off. 'I can find my own way from here.'

'We ain't turning you loose on your own with the Utes all stirred up,' insisted Jed, tying his bedroll to the back of his saddle.

'But they're of my blood,' replied the youngster, using his saddle-horn to swing gracefully up on to his mount. 'My ma's sister to an influential warrior, who's also blood brother to my pa. They'd never do anything to hurt me.'

'Look, kid,' said Jed, 'don't take this unkindly, 'cause I sure don't mean to hurt your feelings none, for you're some spunky kid, but you're a half-breed, and in my experience of dealing with Injuns, when it comes to war, anyone who ain't pure-bred and livin' with 'em is likely to be viewed as fair game.'

'The Utes ain't like that.'

'I hope for your sake you're right, but me and Joe ain't willing to take the chance, so we'll stick with ya until we find your pa.' It was at that precise moment that an arrow swished through the air to bury itself in the trapper's thigh. 'God damn!' he screamed, through his excruciating pain, as a second arrow thudded into the exposed root of a tree inches from where he squirmed defencelessly upon the ground. He tried to remove the brightly banded shaft from his leg, but it was in too deep. 'We're done for.'

Spine-tingling war cries filled the air as a dozen riders galloped into the gully intent on pressing home their advantage. Joe reached for the rifle stowed on his horse, but before he could pull it clear, the spooked animal reared up away from him, causing him to lose his grip on the weapon. Horse and man danced around each other in surreal fashion as the frightened trapper desperately tried to manoeuvre himself into position to make another grab for his gun. Death lay but a heartbeat away. Panic caused him to redouble his efforts to reach the rifle, but as he did so he heard a young voice cry out frantically in a language he did not understand.

'Stop! Stop!' roared Little Hawk, sprinting across the ground to meet the advancing warriors. 'It is me, Little Hawk, the nephew of Wanaka!'

The lead warrior brought his mount to a slithering halt in front of the wild-eyed youngster. All about him angry war cries were dying in the throats of the other warriors as they reined in all about the gulley in response to his raised hand, with frowns and curious looks forming upon their brightly-painted faces.

'What is the son of Curtis McKenzie doing here with these killers of squaws and children?' demanded the leader of the war party.

'These men have killed no one,' insisted the youngster, locking eyes with the warrior, determined not to show any sign of fear. 'They are just trappers, like my father.'

The warrior grunted, irritably. 'We shall see,' he hissed, wheeling his mount about to face the other Utes. 'See if they have any of our ponies or scalps in their belongings.'

His companions swiftly dismounted to do his bidding. When they returned, empty-handed, he was forced to accept that the boy was right.

'These are not the ones we seek. But as it was my intention to kill all the whites we found in our mountains, it is lucky for them that the son of McKenzie was present in their camp this morning. Now tell me why you are here?'

He had little option but to come clean. Just as he feared his honest response caused much merriment amongst the Utes. However, his humiliation was short-lived, for the leader of the war party quickly silenced the hecklers.

'Little Hawk has acted foolishly,' he said. 'He is a boy and should leave such things to men, but no one can doubt your courage, or your loyalty to your mother's people. I think that perhaps, one day, you will make a fine warrior.' Having said his piece, he gave a loud whoop, and led the war party away at a canter through the trees.

Joe moved swiftly to his wounded friend's side, where he was soon joined by Little Hawk. 'I don't know what you said to convince them to leave us be,' he said, 'but me and ole Jed are truly grateful for your quick-thinking. You sure as hell saved our hides.'

'That's all right, Joe,' replied Hawk, bursting with pride. 'How's Jed doing?'

'Oh, Jed's doin' jest fine and dandy,' growled the wounded trapper through clenched teeth, 'considering he's got a damn arrow lodged in his leg.'

'Don't mind him,' advised Joe, nudging Little Hawk with his elbow, 'he ain't never happy unless he's got somit' to complain about.'

'Can you cut it out?' queried the youngster. Joe shook his head.

'No, it's in too deep. If I tried, he'd probably end up bleeding to death. It's a real bad wound, he's gonna need proper doctoring.'

'The nearest one's in Santa Fe, and that's a good four days' ride from here.'

Jed grunted in pain and clenched his fists tightly as Joe snapped off the feathered end of the shaft. After a few minutes, he tried to sit up, but a sudden sharp stab of pain in his thigh forced him back down.

'There ain't no way in hell I'm gonna be able to sit a horse,' he stated, gritting his teeth, 'so how do you propose to get me all the way to Santa Fe?'

In the event, it was Little Hawk who came up with the idea of building an Indian-style travois which would enable the injured man to reach the McKenzie cabin. It took him and Joe no time at all to find, cut and shape the branches they needed. They then fixed the largest, thickest blanket they possessed to the poles, before finally rigging the whole contraption to the back of Joe's horse. An hour and a half after sun-up, they were on their way.

Although it was far from the most comfortable ride Jed had ever experienced, the poles and blanket which bore him along behind his partner's horse stood up to the task admirably. The party travelled slow and easy, to minimize the jarring effects on the trapper's debilitating wound. They had progressed less than a mile from their overnight campsite when a lone rider came into view. It soon became obvious that he was heading straight for them.

'It's my pa,' announced Little Hawk when the approaching rider finally drew close enough to be recognized.

'And he looks madder than a grizzly with a sore tooth!' observed Joe.

An unsmiling McKenzie cantered up to confront Little Hawk and his companions. Having eyed them warily he said, 'I'd say you've seen some trouble.'

'That's a fact,' replied Joe, rubbing the back of his neck. 'My name's Joe Maddocks, and my partner,' he paused briefly to point a thumb back over his shoulder at the man in the litter, 'is Jed Smart. We had a little run in with a Ute war party early this morning.'

'Is that a fact?'

'Yeah, and I'll tell you what, if it hadn't been for that kid of yourn our hair would now be dangling from a war lance.'

Maddocks quickly related the whole story, heaping praise on the shoulders of an embarrassed-looking Hawk. Throughout the trapper's animated account, McKenzie remained motionless and expressionless upon his horse. Only when Joe had said his piece did he finally turn his attention to his errant son.

'Is that the way it happened?' he asked.

'Yeah, pa, more or less.'

'Who was leading the war party?' The boy shrugged his shoulders.

'Some young buck I've never seen before. But he's sure out for blood.'

Cursing under his breath, McKenzie dismounted and strolled over to check on the wounded man in the travois. Jed Smart raised himself up on to his elbows when he caught sight of McKenzie coming around the pack animals, but the awful pain in his thigh caused him to collapse back down on to the litter.

'Excuse me if'n I don't stand up to shake hands, pard,' he said, raising his hand in greeting as his visitor halted directly in front of him.

'Mind if I take a look?' asked McKenzie, nodding towards the broken shaft protruding from the man's upper leg.

'Be my guest.'

McKenzie could see the trapper had lost a lot of blood. The area around where the point of the arrow was embedded was badly swollen and discoloured, a clear indication that infection had set in. Unless the wounded man received prompt medical attention, he would lose the leg, if not his life.

'It's a bad one, ain't it?' said Jed Smart when he saw McKenzie shake his head.

'Yeah. We need to get that arrow head out, and sooner rather than later.'

'Can you cut it out?' asked Maddocks, resting his arm against the flank of the horse that supported the travois. McKenzie shook his head.

'No, but my wife could, she's better than any white doctor I've ever met. She's a natural-born healer. We'll head for my place.'

'We're obliged to you,' said Maddocks. He grunted respectfully in response to the iron grip that pumped his outstretched hand. 'And to your son, too, he's quite a kid.'

'That he is,' agreed McKenzie, glaring at his anxious-looking offspring. 'Though he still needs to learn to do as he's told. You could have got yourself killed.'

'I know,' replied the chastened youngster, shame registering on his reddening face. 'I'm sorry, pa, I wasn't thinking straight. It's just. . . .'

'Just what?'

'Well, when you rode off after Josie I figured the trail would go cold if I didn't do something, and I just couldn't bear the thought of those murderers getting clean away.'

'You can't fault his good intentions,' interjected Maddocks, hauling himself up into the saddle. 'Or his spunk.'

'No, I can't,' agreed McKenzie, putting an arm around his son's shoulders to guide him back to his pony. 'But good intentions ain't gonna save him from a trip to the woodshed when I get him home.'

'I got it coming,' admitted Little Hawk.

There was a twinkle in Maddocks' eye when he pushed his coonskin cap further back on to his greying head. It was obvious that he had something pressing on his mind.

'I ain't never been one for interfering in another man's business, less'n I could avoid it,' he said. 'And I would certainly never presume to tell you how to deal with your own young'un, but if you're aiming to give him a licking for doing what he did, then you'll have to go through me to reach that woodshed of yourn.' McKenzie smiled broadly.

'Now that might make for an interesting contest,'

he observed, light-heartedly.

'The way I figure it, your wife will have her hands full with Jed here, I don't think she'll be too happy about patching us up, too,' said Maddocks.

'You got a point,' conceded McKenzie, swinging about to grin up at his son. 'So maybe I'll settle for a month of chores instead of a whupping.'

8

McKenzie's faith in his wife's ability to successfully treat the injured trapper's ugly wound proved well founded. She operated with all the skill of an army surgeon, and a minimum of fuss, only pausing to offer her patient an occasional kindly word of reassurance. As he lay on the kitchen table, biting down on a piece of stick, she deftly cut out the arrow head with a sharp knife, before cleaning the damaged tissue with a dash of whiskey from the bottle her husband kept for medicinal purposes.

'You're running a slight fever,' she said, as she stitched the gaping hole in his leg. 'I'll need to keep an eye on you for a few days, but you should heal up fine.'

'Pardon my language, ma'am,' chirped his partner, 'but I have to say, you're one hell of a doctor.'

Jed Smart gleefully, if somewhat stiffly, accepted the whiskey bottle from McKenzie with a nod of thanks as he gingerly swung his legs over the edge of the table. The pleasant burning sensation in the back of his throat caused him to cough lightly and certainly helped to take his mind off the throbbing pain in his thigh. He surveyed the sparsely furnished cabin through watery eyes. A Hawkins rifle sat astride a pair of wooden pegs on the wall above the fire which crackled and blazed in the stone hearth beneath, but the most striking feature bar none was the huge bearskin hanging right beside the solid door to his left.

'That must have taken some separating from its previous owner,' he quipped, with an admiring nod towards the trophy, as he handed the bottle back to his host.

'It was him or me,' said McKenzie. 'He caught me completely unawares while I was setting traps in a stream up west of here. I just managed to get my shot off in time, though it didn't pleasure me none to do it. A grizzly is one of God's finest critters and they're deserving of our respect rather than a bullet between the eyes.'

'You don't talk like any mountain man I ever met,' observed Joe Maddocks. 'Those I know regard any furry creature as fair game.'

McKenzie knew he was right, but then he prided himself in being different from other men. Sure, he trapped for profit and killed for food and clothing, in order to survive, but he was openly contemptuous of those who indulged in pointless trophy-hunting or displays of bravado. His views and outlook on life had been greatly influenced by the curious, friendly Utes who had welcomed him into their camps and shaped his outlook on life during his early, formative months in the high country.

The Indians had patiently taught him the value of living with nature rather than merely off it. Their friendship and guidance enabled him to master their language and the skills he needed to survive in the savage wilderness: how to read sign or a change in the weather; the best way to build a shelter; where to find the best beaver ponds; and the need to respect the numerous four-legged predators, large and small, with whom they shared the land.

He nodded at his smiling wife as she exited through the door to empty the bloody water from the bowl she had used to clean the mountain man's wound.

'She's quite a gal,' observed Jed Smart, limping over to sit in the home-made chair by the fire, 'and pretty as a picture.'

McKenzie nodded. His mind wandered back to the day he had first set eyes on the only daughter of Grey Bull.

Bright Star in The Morning Sky was how the shy, demure girl was known to her people. During his first visit to trade in her father's camp, the sixteen year old had kept a wary eye on the hairy white man as she helped her mother around the tepee. Every time he had caught her peeking at him, he had simply smiled back in a friendly fashion. When he had left that day he gave her a present, a comb for her long, shiny, raven-black hair. On his next visit some weeks later, the grinning girl had presented him with a bear-tooth necklace. He had worn it around his neck ever since.

During his further visits to the encampment, McKenzie became totally captivated by her beauty and girlish charms. Furtive little glances and occasional fleeting smiles around the camp fire were soon followed by 'chance' meetings in the hills where she collected berries for her busy mother. One smile from her lips was sufficient to send his heart soaring. He was head over heels in love and knew he had to take her for his wife.

Despite his growing friendship with Grey Bull, the Indian was initially opposed to their union. His daughter had already caught the eye of a number of worthy young warriors within the village and, given the choice, he would have preferred her to marry one of her own people. When, in an uncharacteristic show of rebellion for a Ute girl, she insisted she truly loved the bearded white man and would accept no other for her husband, her father finally relented and gave his consent, in return for a Hawkins rifle and a Bowie knife.

Their love for each other continued to blossom with each passing year. Little Hawk's birth early in the second year of their marriage brought even greater joy into their lives.

They were blissfully happy and wanted for nothing in their own little private corner of paradise. True, it was not an easy life: one careless slip in an icy stream, a chance encounter with a Shoshone raiding party, or any other number of hazards could have claimed his life at any time, but it was the path that he had chosen, and because of that, he was truly a man at peace with himself and God. He wanted nothing more than to be left alone to watch his son grow into adulthood. The trouble was, there were other people who didn't share his feelings for the land or the Indians, and they seemed hell bent on destroying everything in their path.

The whites who had brought death and destruction to a peaceful Ute village fell into that category, but they weren't the only ones. He knew that America was a nation on the move. Like an unstoppable wind, the country was expanding its borders to all the far-flung corners of the vast continent. There was gold in California and rich, fertile farming land to be had for free in Oregon. The trickle of people moving west would eventually become an irresistible tide.

Although the vast bulk of the population still lived east of the mighty Mississippi river, hundreds had already upped stakes and moved west. For the present, their eyes were fixed firmly on California and Oregon, but inevitably there would come a time when some would choose to settle in the high country, rather than merely pass through. There was good land to be had, thousands of square miles, well stocked with timber, water and minerals. The fact that it had already been claimed by another people would count for nothing.

It grieved him to think about how the character of the land itself, not to mention the lives of those who lived upon it, would inevitably change when the miners, loggers and town builders finally arrived. The newcomers would cut down the forests, tear up the land and erect fences, all in the name of progress. For the dispossessed, the Utes and mountain men, it would herald the destruction of everything they held sacred.

'You didn't hear a single word I said, did ya?'

'Huh?' queried McKenzie, staring into the amused face of Joe Maddocks.

'Thought as much,' he chortled. 'I was jest sayin' that since ole Jed is gonna be laid in your barn for a spell, maybe you and I could try running them murderers to ground.' McKenzie shook his head.

'Yesterday's rain will have washed away all evidence of their passing,' he insisted, 'more's the pity. No, we'll just have to hope they run into one of those Ute war parties.'

'It could be that a few honest trappers will lose their hair this summer.'

'That's why I'm planning to ride over to see Grey Bull in the morning. I'm hoping he'll be willing to speak out at the council fires to help keep any young hotheads in check.'

'Well in that case,' said Maddocks, scratching an itch at the back of his neck, 'maybe I can take care of a few chores around here while you're parleying with your Ute friends, just to help repay your hospitality.'

'Thanks,' replied McKenzie, with a twinkle in his eye, 'but my two young'uns sort of volunteered to take care of all the work around here for the next few weeks, to make up for all the trouble they've caused me of late.'

'Well I can't just sit around on my rump,' argued Maddocks, good-naturedly.

'There's nothing to stop you setting some traps, and I can sure tell you where to find some excellent beaver ponds.'

'What about the Utes?'

'They won't bother you none, not now Hawk's spoke up for you.'

'Fair enough then,' agreed Maddocks, 'I'll do as you suggest, but I insist on sharing anything I catch with you.'

'That's mighty neighbourly of you, friend,' said McKenzie, nodding his appreciation as he moved towards the door. 'Now if'n you'll excuse me for a moment, I'd better go check on how the kids are making out with their chores.'

'They don't seem to get along too well,' observed Jed Smart, trying to make himself more comfortable in the chair.

'No, they don't,' agreed his host. 'I just hope things'll improve when they get used to the idea of living together.'

The children had completely ignored each other since Hawk's return, a point which hadn't been lost on their father. McKenzie hoped the onerous task of turning the huge pile of logs by the barn into kindling for the fire would help to break the ice between them. When the only sound he heard was that of the heavy axe splitting timber, he knew his plan had failed.

They had their backs turned to him and were unaware of his presence when he halted by the corner of the building. Little Hawk gave a low grunt and held out the axe to indicate that it was his sister's turn to break sweat. She accepted the razor sharp tool with a scowl and an irritated sigh, before carefully setting the nearest log on its end in front of her. Raising the axe high into the air with both hands, she brought it crashing down only for her rapidly-tiring arms to miss their intended target. Little Hawk burst out laughing when the metal head of the axe sank fast into one of the logs in the main pile directly in front of his embarrassed sister.

'You're utterly useless,' he sneered, 'just like all girls.'

Having shoved her roughly aside, he put his foot on the log and pulled the chopper clear with a smug grin. Before he knew what was happening, the wiry girl sprang at him with all the speed and grace of a big cat. They ended up on the ground, rolling over and over in the dirt, struggling to establish supremacy. Josie's slight weight advantage soon enabled her to get her younger sibling's head in a painful, vice-like grip. Fortunately for him, their pa intervened before he came to any serious harm.

'Quit it!' he roared, hauling his feuding offspring

back to their feet. He stood rock-steady between them, maintaining a firm grip on their arms to prevent them from renewing hostilities. 'What's got into the both of yus?'

'He started it!' snarled Josie, spitting fire.

'You're a liar!' retorted Little Hawk, straining to reach his sister.

'I ain't gonna tell you two again,' warned their pa, shaking them violently by the arm. 'Now just simmer down.'

'I hate you,' growled Little Hawk, glaring at Josie. 'Why did you have to come here?'

Tears instantly welled up in his sister's eyes. With a determined effort, she pulled herself free of her pa's tight grip and ran off towards the stream, some twenty yards distant, where she sat down on the ground with her back up against a tree and started to cry.

'Wait here,' said McKenzie, letting go of his son's arm. 'And don't dare move an inch until I return.' Little Hawk nodded, retrieved the axe with a sigh, and began to take out his frustration on the remaining logs.

Josie steadfastly refused to look up at her pa when she heard him squat down beside her. Tears trickled slowly down her cheeks to land silently in the tall grass. Although he had displayed some kindness and charity towards her since bringing her back, she still felt unwanted, uncomfortable, unhappy, angry and confused. It just wasn't fair, nothing was turning out the way she had expected. Instead of having her pa to herself, she had inherited a whole new family, one who clearly resented her as much as she did them. Star had largely ignored her, even when they had been left alone together, while Little Hawk's open hostility had inevitably led to a fight.

The light breeze gently ruffled her hair and the grass along the stream. She looked at her pa through moist, glistening eyes and said, 'Why do Hawk and Star hate me so?'

'They don't hate you, Josie,' he replied, frowning.

'Little Hawk does,' she sighed. 'He said as much.'

'He didn't really mean it,' insisted her pa, 'he's just mad at you for showing him up. He ain't used to getting his tail whipped by no girl.'

'I would have given him a black eye for sure if you hadn't pulled me off him,' she admitted. 'I guess I should go apologize for being so mean.' McKenzie shook his head.

'No need; he had it coming for teasing you the way he did.'

'What about Star? She hardly said two words to me all the while you were out looking for Hawk. I reckon she blames me for him taking off the way he did.'

'Well, you were indirectly responsible for his folly,' said McKenzie. 'Your running off like a thief in the night prevented me from going after the men who raided the Utes. It gave that little scamp all the excuse he needed to go play at being a man.'

'I'm sorry, I promise I'll never run away again.'

'OK,' he said. 'And don't worry about Star, she'll forgive you soon enough. We all need to bend a little and make a few adjustments in order to make this thing work – you, me, Star and that new brother of yourn. We have to get to know each other properly, get comfortable around each other, then we'll make out just fine. Star said as much herself.'

'She did?'

'Yeah,' he said, helping his daughter to her feet. 'Now I need to have a word with Hawk, so you run along to the cabin and get washed up for supper.'

'You're not going to punish him for starting the fight are you?' she asked. 'It wouldn't be right, it was as much my doing as his.'

'Stickin' up fer your brother, eh?' he said, patting her on the shoulder. 'Now that's what I call an encouraging sign. But there ain't no need for you to go worrying your sweet head none over Hawk. Him and I just need to get a few things straight, that's all.'

Having walked Josie halfway to the house, McKenzie veered off towards the barn, where he found his son still hard at work splitting logs. He stuck out a hand to take the axe from his sweaty palms and then went to work on the last few remaining logs.

'Good job,' he said, 'I reckon we've enough firewood to see us through to winter.'

Hawk could tell from his pa's easy, relaxed demeanour that he wasn't going to wail the tar out of him for goading Josie into a fight, even though his behaviour might have warranted it. He didn't like his new sister, and was mad at his pa for bringing her into their lives, but he still knew that he had no call to act that way.

'I shouldn't have said what I did,' he admitted, too ashamed to look his pa in the eye.

'No, you're right about that, son. Josie's having a pretty rough time of it right now, and you ain't helping.'

'No one asked her to come here.'

McKenzie put an arm around his son's shoulders. 'Nobody asked her ma to die either. She had nowhere else to go, Hawk, and now she's become a stranger in a strange land where she's hurting, scared and confused. Just imagine how you would feel if you were suddenly uprooted from the mountains and taken to live in a city with folks you'd never met.'

'I'd just die,' he conceded.

'This is tough on me, too, you know. Until a few days ago I didn't even know I had a daughter. You and your ma were my whole world; now, like I just told Josie, we've all got to make some adjustments and learn to get along.'

'But I don't even like her!'

'You might, if you give her a chance,' advised his pa. 'Though I'll admit, she does take some getting used to.'

'Do you like her?'

'Yeah, I guess I do,' replied McKenzie. 'I'm kinda getting used to the idea of having her around. She reminds me of you, what with her stubborn streak and all. Just cut her some slack. Whether you like it or not, she's here to stay, and nothing's gonna change that. She's a part of our family now, and we have to stick together, no matter what.'

'OK,' he sighed. 'I'll try, but it won't be easy.'

'Who said anything about it being easy?' asked McKenzie, shepherding his son towards the cabin. 'But I'm still relying on you to do the right thing.'

9

Under normal circumstances, Joe Maddocks would have been simply mortified at the prospect of having a pair of kids tag along while he explored the beaver country close to McKenzie's cabin. Kids were excess baggage and a right pain in the ass to boot! It was one reason why he had refrained from taking himself an Indian wife. However, when his genial host had muted the idea of his feuding offspring accompanying him, Maddocks had almost bitten his hand off in gratitude.

In spite of McKenzie's assertion that the Utes wouldn't bother him, he felt somewhat uneasy about wandering too far from the relative security of the peaceful valley. His unexpected run in with the Indians had left him rather wary, but Little Hawk's presence offered the guarantee of safe passage. The boy also knew the territory like the back of his hand and was able to guide him straight as an arrow to the best beaver ponds.

Josie and Hawk were also pleased with the arrangement, despite the prevailing tension between them. A day's trapping in the mountains was viewed as preferable to the endless, tiresome chores their pa had in mind following their collective misdemeanours.

For the most part, they rode in silence, revelling in the warm sun on their backs and the gentle kiss of the south wind. Spring had brought its annual touch of freshness and new life to the high country. Josie quietly took in the majesty of it all in from astride her pony: the spectacular panoramas; the clean air; gurgling streams; a deer with its fawn; the chilling howl of a lone wolf hidden in the dark forest; the song of a lark high above her head and the light breeze gently rippling through the colourful array of pretty flowers and lush green grass on the hillsides. She felt as if she was in her own private corner of paradise. No wonder her pa loved this country.

An hour into their expedition, as the riders paralleled the course of a narrow stream, they entered a box-canyon whose beauty surpassed anything Josie had ever seen in her entire life. At the far end of the canyon a spectacular waterfall tumbled down from the high cliffs to form a deep, wide rock pool.

'Good beaver country,' announced Maddocks, standing tall in his stirrups to excitedly survey the scene. He nodded happily at Hawk. 'You've done me proud, boy.' Kicking his mount into motion and pulling on the rope tied to the pack mule, which carried all the tools of his trade, he led the way into the canyon.

When they reached the rock pool at the base of the falls, the children quickly helped the mountain man unload his gear. They then saw to the animals, leaving Maddocks free to explore the vicinity and set his traps.

'I'm going to see if I can lend him a hand,' said Hawk, when they had picketed the animals close to water and good grazing. 'Are you coming?' Josie shook her head.

'No, I reckon I'll just stay here and sit a spell,' she replied, squatting down on a rock.

'Suit yourself,' he said, shrugging his shoulders, 'but we'll be a while.'

She waved her hand dismissively and gazed up into the bright heavens in response to the eerie cry of a hawk, gracefully circling the valley on a current of air. When it finally disappeared from sight beyond the craggy peaks of the snow-capped mountains to the east, she came to her feet suddenly attracted by the idea of exploring the forest.

Although it felt slightly chilly out of the sun, she pressed on ever further into the depths of the woods, whistling contentedly to herself. Pine needles crunched beneath her feet as she wove her way through the trees, relishing the sweet, pungent aroma of damp, rotting vegetation and the antics of the numerous noisy squirrels in the branches of the tall trees. After a while though, the rustling of the leaves in the wind caused her to feel slightly ill at ease, prompting her to retrace her steps.

Hawk and Maddocks were nowhere to be seen when Josie reached the picketed animals. With a sigh and a shrug of her shoulders, she set off in search of them. Almost immediately, as she rounded a bend in the trail, the astonished little girl came face to face with a bear fishing in the stream. It was hard to tell who was more startled, Josie or the black bear wading in the shallow water. When the reality of the situation finally hit her, Josie let out a piercing, terrified scream and took to her heels. While it was an instinctive and understandable reaction, it was a very ill-advised one, for it prompted the bear to give chase.

With legs pumping like a pair of pistons, Josie bolted along the bank of the stream. The sound of heavy, pounding, clawed feet and menacing, throaty snarls from the rear confirmed the critter was hot on her heels. In desperation, she veered off into the trees hoping to outmanoeuvre the beast in the dense undergrowth. Unfortunately for her, the bear was far more at home in the forest than any greenhorn kid from the east.

By constantly twisting and turning between the tall evergreens, she managed to evade the bear's clutches. Her lungs felt like they were on fire and her heart was about ready to burst, but adrenalin and fear kept her tiring legs moving. She had no idea where she was going or how long she could survive, given the creature's grim determination to get up close and personal. It was reminiscent of the games of tag she had once played with her friends back on the farm, but a lot more dangerous, for capture meant certain death rather than a childish forfeit.

She was surprised at the cumbersome-looking critter's dexterity and stamina. Although she gained a few precious yards each time she skilfully used the trunks of the mighty pines to change direction, the bear's superior speed and sure-footedness soon enabled it to close the gap again within seconds. Twice its razor sharp claws came within a mere whisker of bringing her down. The petrified youngster's high-pitched squeals echoed through the still air, putting birds and a host of small game to flight, as she continued to plough a desperate, zig-zag course through the wild, undulating terrain.

No suitable bolthole presented itself during her panic-inspired dash through the woods and the bear remained too close for her to risk stopping to shin up a tree. She knew that she couldn't run for ever; sooner, rather than later, her aching legs or heaving lungs, or both, would give out. Then the bear would instantly pounce to rip her apart. Only a stubborn will to survive kept her moving.

As she neared the edge of the thinning woods an idea suddenly popped into her head. The rock pool was close by. If she could reach it in time, there was a chance the wide, deep water might offer an avenue of escape. Hope generated fresh energy. She deftly hurdled a fallen tree lying directly in her path and burst out into the open making a beeline for the pool some twenty yards distant.

Less than halfway to her objective, with the enraged animal almost literally breathing down her neck, there came a sudden peculiar swishing sound, quickly followed by another. The bear tumbled forward with a muffled, throaty roar to sweep the screaming girl off her feet. She crashed landed face-up on the grassy bank with the bear's snarling head draped across her legs. The beast's heavy body shuddered once, twice, then fell limp. It was only then that Josie became aware of the two feathered shafts protruding from its chest.

'Will you quit fooling around with the wildlife, we've work to do,' called Little Hawk from the edge of the woods as he lowered his bow and strolled casually over to join his white-faced sister. With a concerted effort she managed to pull her bruised and scratched limbs clear of the dead beast, irritably slapping away his offer of a hand up. 'There's gratitude for you,' he said, 'I save your miserable hide and you get all uppity.'

'Just shut up!' she snapped, trembling all over as tears welled up in her eyes.

'There ain't no need to start crying, you're safe now. It's dead, it can't hurt ya none.'

'Who's crying?' she wailed.

'You are,' he replied.

'That's only 'cause I've got something in my eye,'

she stated, pretending to remove a speck of dirt.

'Sure you have,' he replied, placing his bow across his shoulders. 'Well the least you could do is say thanks.'

'Thanks!' she exclaimed, loudly for effect. Little Hawk shook his head and sighed.

'I don't know why I bothered,' he said, proudly giving the downed bear a satisfied kick. The smirk on his face vanished in a trice when his keen ears picked up the sound of someone hurrying towards them. As he reached for his bow the panting figure of Joe Maddocks arrived on the scene.

'You missed all the fun, Joe. My sister tried to get herself eaten by a bear,' he said, lowering his weapon.

'Good grief, boy,' said Joe, 'two arrows right in the heart. Now that's some shooting! Where'd you ever learn to handle a bow like that?'

'My Ute relatives taught me.' When he started boasting about how he could out-shoot any Ute boy his age, Josie felt obliged to put him in his place.

'Pity they never saw fit to teach ya to wrestle,' she quipped. Her barbed comment had the desired effect; it stung his pride. The look upon his face as their eyes met, coupled with the clenching of his fists, suggested a rematch was imminent. Maddocks read his intentions.

'I've finishing setting my traps, so let me give you a hand skinning your kill, son,' he said merrily, laying a restraining hand upon his shoulder. 'It ought'a look good on the wall alongside the one your pa shot, or maybe you'd rather have it for a blanket. Keep you mighty warm come winter.'

'OK,' said Hawk, making an effort to control his anger. 'Let's get it done.'

The sheer size of the brute meant that it took the pair of them working in tandem nearly half an hour to complete the task. Josie watched them from a discreet distance. She had no wish to get close to the bear again, even though it could no longer do her any harm. When they had finished their bloody labours, the mountain man bundled the skin up and tied it to the back of the mule.

Little Hawk was keen to explore another favourite spot deep in the mountains, three miles further north, which he insisted would yield rich pickings. With plenty of daylight remaining, and a handful of snares still at his disposal, Maddocks gave his approval to the idea, but insisted on stopping for a bite of late lunch first.

The children were promptly despatched to find kindling for a fire. Maddocks had three huge steaks cut up and ready for grilling by the time they returned. When Josie realized to her horror that bear meat was on the menu, she immediately lost her appetite. Unlike her grinning male companions, she refused to see the funny side of eating something that had been all set to chew on her! Even the succulent aroma drifting through the air failed to change her mind, despite the rumbling in her empty tummy.

Josie's close encounter with the bear and her stubborn refusal to feast on its defeated carcass made her the butt of many a joke throughout the afternoon. At first she took it in good part, but eventually their antics proved tiresome, at which point she fell back behind them in a sullen sulk. However, she made sure she always kept them in sight, just in case any other critters took a fancy to chomping on a defenceless little white girl.

Josie chose to maintain her brooding silence throughout the afternoon, even when Maddocks, realizing they had gotten under her skin, made every effort to mend fences. All his cheery attempts to win her over, both while he was setting the rest of his traps and on the ride home, fell on deaf ears.

For his part, Little Hawk wisely opted to keep his distance. He sensed that if he let his guard down and strayed too near, she would find some excuse for resorting to fisticuffs to settle her grievances. Not that he was scared of her or anything, but he didn't see the sense in fighting over something as trivial as her inability to see the funny side of a joke. There was also the small matter of what their pa would say if he found out they'd had another scrap. He felt sure that after the lecture of the night before, he would get saddled with all the blame, and the licking he had narrowly avoided on more than one occasion of late, would inevitably follow as surely as night follows day. It was not a price he was prepared to pay.

The sound of their approaching horses in the fading light brought McKenzie to the door of the cabin. A relieved smile flickered across his face, for when they had failed to return by sunset, he'd become a trifle concerned, even allowing for the fact that Maddocks was no tenderfoot. There were inherent risks attached to travelling in the mountains, at any time of year: a sudden change in the weather; accident; illness, and attacks by wild animals or Indians had accounted for many a good man. Few trappers lived to enjoy old age. Those who did were generally crippled by arthritis or rheumatism from the years they spent fighting the elements or wading through freezing streams to set their traps.

'I was getting worried,' he said, strolling across to join the three riders as they dismounted by the barn. 'Did you run into some trouble?'

Maddocks smiled, rested his arms against his saddle, then motioned with his head towards the trophy strapped across the back of his mule. 'Nothing we couldn't handle.' He then happily related, in typical mountain man fashion, an exaggerated account of the incident with the bear, praising Little Hawk to the hilt for his swift, courageous and decisive action in rescuing his sister.

Josie's scowl as she led her pony into the barn suggested there was more to the story than McKenzie had been told, and he said as much.

'She's mad 'cause we teased her some about not wanting to eat bear meat,' confessed Maddocks, removing his coonskin hat in order to scratch his head. 'I guess we went too far, though I did try to apologize on the way home, but she weren't having none of it.'

'That sounds like my daughter,' said McKenzie, smiling ruefully. He inclined his head towards his son, who had his hands full in unloading the bear skin from the mule. 'What about you, Hawk? Have you said sorry to Josie, too?'

'No way!' exclaimed the youngster, depositing his bear pelt proudly on the ground. 'I ain't going within a mile of her until she calms down.'

'That probably makes sense,' agreed his pa. 'But I do expect you to make your peace with her come morning.'

'I saved her life, why should I have to say sorry as well, just for having a little fun?' The stern look upon his pa's face convinced him to adopt a slightly more conciliatory stance. 'OK,' he sighed, unsaddling his pony, 'I'll apologize, but if she slugs me, I'll hit her right back and hang the consequences.'

10

Hawk tried to make good on his promise to apologise to Josie right after breakfast the following morning. 'Are you OK?' he asked as they collected water from the stream.

'Huh?' she frowned, swinging the empty pail in her hands. When he repeated the question she laughed and said, 'What do you care?'

Not for the first time he was sorely tempted to box her ears, but he thought better of it. On reaching the stream, he took the bucket from her and dipped it into the clear water. He accidentally splashed some ice-cold water over her bare feet as he withdrew the pail from the stream. His quick apology only added to Josie's impression that he had done it deliberately. She glared at him, hands on hips.

'I'm sorry,' he insisted, 'I was jest clumsy. I didn't do it on purpose, honest.' When he heard a trout jump in the stream, he turned away to watch its progress. In an instant he was sitting on the bank removing his moccasins.

'What are you doing now?' she queried. He put a finger to his lips.

'Shush. Jest keep quiet for a moment and you'll be eating trout for lunch.'

He rolled his britches up over his knees and then waded out carefully into the chilly waters, directly ahead of the unsuspecting fish. He stood rock still, legs wide apart, hands poised for action, eyes unwaveringly focused on the approaching trout. As it passed between his legs he scooped it up in two hands, yelling with glee. Its slippery scales made it difficult for him to gain any purchase, and as a result the trout was able to jump clear of his flailing hands. When he tried to wade after it, he lost his balance and fell face first into the water.

Josie burst out laughing. 'Some fisherman you are!' she exclaimed, slapping her side.

'I'd like to see you do any better,' he said, wading slowly back to shore.

Never one to turn her back on a challenge, Josie promptly rolled her britches up and entered the stream. It wasn't long before another fair-sized trout appeared on the scene.

'Don't stand where you'll cast a shadow,' warned Hawk.

'I know what I'm doing,' she insisted, carefully adjusting her position. She made three unsuccessful grabs for the fish and then gave up in disgust. 'It ain't as easy as it looks,' she admitted as they returned to the house, carrying the pail between them.

'Look at the state of you! You've been fighting again,' said their pa when they entered the cabin. Their damp and dishevelled appearance caused him to jump to the wrong conclusion. 'Which one of you started it this time?'

Josie just could not resist such a heaven-sent opportunity to have a little fun at her brother's expense. 'He did,' she said, as they lowered the pail of water to the floor. 'He always does, don't he?'

Her totally unexpected response left Hawk momentarily dumbstruck. His face was a mixture of astonishment and impotent rage. He stared incredulously at his pa, lost for words.

'You're in big trouble, boy,' said his pa, coming to his feet.

'But I didn't do anything!' exclaimed Hawk. 'She's lying.'

'I am not!' insisted Josie, trying hard to maintain a straight face while sounding all indignant. 'He threw a bucket of water over me.'

'Well, Hawk,' demanded his pa, 'what do you have to say for yourself?'

The youngster's shoulders sagged in defeat. He knew his crafty, spiteful sister had set him up for a fall by pretending to befriend him. Nothing he could say would save his hide. His pa was going to take her word for it and that was that. His knuckles turned white as he glared at his smug looking sister. He felt a sudden urge to wring her scrawny little neck. Then, quite unexpectedly she suddenly burst out laughing.

'I'm sorry, pa,' she sniggered, 'but I just couldn't resist paying Hawk back for all the grief he caused me yesterday. We didn't really get into a fight, we got wet trying to catch a trout in the stream.'

'Haw, haw, haw!' roared Jed Smart from his seat by the fire. 'She sure got you good that time, boy. But if'n it had been me, I'd have waited until your pa wailed the tar out of ya before I'd have spoken up!'

'I was sorely tempted,' admitted Josie with a grin.

Everyone, except her brother, of course, was highly amused. He didn't appreciate being on the receiving end of her joke one little bit, which was why he stormed out of the house in a huff, slamming the door behind him.

'Where are you going?' asked McKenzie when he saw Josie heading for the door.

'To make my peace with Hawk,' she said over her shoulder. 'I know what it feels like to have everyone laughing at you.'

'But we weren't laughing at him, we was laughing at you!' exclaimed Joe Maddocks. 'That was some trick you played on him.'

'I'd stay well clear of him until he cools down,' warned her pa. 'He'll be fighting mad right now.'

'I can handle him,' insisted Josie loudly as she disappeared outside.

She found him sitting cross-legged on a bale of straw in the barn. He didn't say a word when she climbed up backwards on to the top rail of a nearby stall.

'That wasn't something I planned,' she said. 'It just sort of happened.'

'You was being mean,' he snapped. 'Pa was all set to give me a licking.'

'I wouldn't have let that happen,' she said. 'I was just having some fun, that's all. I kinda wanted to even the score for what happened yesterday.'

'Why'd you follow me out here?' She shrugged her shoulders.

'I guess I wanted to say sorry. Look, now we're even, can't we make a go of getting along? It seems to me that we're stuck with each other, like it or not, and things'll be better all round if we try to get along.'

'But I don't like you,' he snapped.

'And I ain't exactly fond of you either,' she retorted, 'but pa says we have a month of chores ahead of us for all the trouble we've caused, so maybe if we work together we might get to know each other better and become a mite more friendly. What do you say?'

'OK,' he agreed, rising from his seat. 'Let's give peace a chance.'

11

A full month after the incident with the Utes, Jed Smart's wounded thigh had mended well enough for him to become self-sufficient. After some discussion with his partner, the trappers decided to return to their favoured streams deep in Shoshone country. In spite of McKenzie's confident reassurances that they would encounter no further trouble with the Utes, Smart still felt somewhat nervous about remaining in unfamiliar territory all the while the merest hint of trouble hung on the breeze.

On the morning of their departure they packed their gear and then walked their horses over to the small corral where McKenzie stood silently leaning against the top rail, watching his children cleaning out the chicken coop.

Josie and Hawk had toiled quite amicably side by side, week after week, without one word of complaint, on the various tasks their pa had set them. They had sweated, strained, talked and, sometimes, even laughed together as they mended fences, weeded the small corn field to the rear of the cabin, fed and watered the stock and cleaned their pa's evil-looking beaver traps. There were still occasional disagreements, but none that had led to blows. Their relationship was blossoming all the time. Mutual respect and tolerance were now being supplemented by the first genuine signs of warmth. It was exactly what their pa had been hoping for when he'd set their punishment.

'Now they are laughing together,' said Star as she joined her husband and the trappers by the corral, where he was pretending to clean a horse bridle while observing the youngsters collect eggs from the chicken coop. 'They are friends, just like you said they would be.'

'No,' he replied, shaking his head, 'not yet they ain't. One swallow don't make a summer. They're sort'a feeling each other out, testing the water, so to speak.'

'But at least they've stopped fighting,' she insisted. 'And that's a good sign.'

'Yeah,' he agreed. 'But then I knew they would. They just needed time together. Heck, I still hardly know Josie myself, but I tell you what, she's a game gal.'

Star smiled at her husband as he dropped the bridle he had been polishing and pulled her into a warm embrace. Their unexpected moment of innocent passion caused Joe Maddocks and his partner much amusement.

'You planning on coming up for air?' queried Jed Smart with a chuckle.

McKenzie slowly disentangled himself from his wife's arms with a warm smile. 'You all set to take off?' he asked. Smart nodded. 'Then I wish you good hunting, friends.' He extended his hand to each of the trappers in turn.

'Could be we'll run into each other at rendezvous next month,' said Maddocks, easing himself up into the saddle of his big bay mare, sporting a broad grin on his heavily-bearded face. 'If 'n so, I'm of a mind to buy you a drink, or maybe ten or twelve.'

'I'll keep an eye out for you,' promised McKenzie with a wave as the men turned their mounts towards the trail that led out of the secluded valley. 'Watch your top-knots!' The trappers waved back as they headed out at a trot, pausing briefly to say goodbye to the children.

'How about we go visit your family?' asked McKenzie, as their guests finally rode away. 'I think it's time Josie got to meet her Ute neighbours.'

'I am not sure she will want to go,' replied Star.

'Who say's she'll be given any choice in the matter?' said McKenzie, mischievously. As it turned out, Josie didn't turn a hair when her pa broke the news. For once, whatever anxieties she still harboured about wild Indians took second place to natural curiosity about their habitat and lifestyle. Besides, to have displayed fear or caused a fuss would have made her lose face in front of Hawk, and that was not something she was prepared to contemplate. Instead, she happily helped her new mother pack provisions for the trip.

They reached the Ute encampment late in the afternoon. The first thing that struck Josie as they approached the closely-grouped tepees was the overpowering, unpleasant smell that assailed her nostrils, a curious mixture of human waste and stale food. It made her want to gag, but she tried to breathe normally in the hope that she would quickly become accustomed to the stench all about her. The other thing she noticed as they rode on into the village was the fact that the women were doing all the work while the men sat around the stone fire-circles talking and smoking.

'No different to our towns,' she mumbled to herself as McKenzie brought them to a halt in front of a brightly-decorated tepee in the centre of the village.

'It is my brother's home,' said Star, smiling at Josie as she slipped off the back of her horse. 'Come child, don't be nervous, we are welcome here.'

In spite of Star's words of reassurance and the comforting, towering presence of her father, Josie no longer felt so blasé about the visit. The sea of curious bronzed faces round about, coupled with the smell and squalor of the camp caused her to swallow hard as she tentatively eased herself out of the saddle. Hawk couldn't help but grin when he saw his half-sister step forward to cling on tight to the sleeve of their pa's fringed, buckskin jacket. It was obvious from her demeanour that she felt rather uncomfortable and totally out of her element. He decided to turn this to his advantage, if and when a suitable opportunity arose. They might be getting along OK these days, but he still felt he owed her in some small measure for all the trouble she had caused him in the past.

Star's family were very pleased to see their visitors and made a real fuss of them, especially Josie, whose facial expressions when tasting unfamiliar fare during dinner caused great merriment. Hawk was able to have a lot of fun at her expense during whispered conversations with his many young Ute cousins round the fire after the meal. With everyone happily chattering away in a language she did not understand, Josie soon felt left out of things. The laughter from her brother and his friends, coupled with the odd furtive glance in her direction, told her all she needed to know about what they were discussing, and this only served to make her increasingly sullen and withdrawn as the evening wore on. Having made every effort to be pleasant to her irritating little half-brother ever since promising her pa she would try to get along with him, she quite naturally felt hurt by his rather insensitive actions. By the time they all turned in for the night she had only one thing in mind: revenge.

By morning, as the children strolled side by side down to the stream to wash, Josie's temper had cooled sufficiently for her to put all thoughts of retribution out of her mind. However, she still felt obliged to give her brother a piece of her mind.

'Don' think I don't know what you and your cousins were up to last night,' she said, kneeling down beside the gently-flowing stream to splash cold water onto her sleepy face.

'What are you talking about, Josie?' retorted Hawk, feigning puzzlement.

'You were being mean to me and you know it.'

'You're crazy, girl, we were doing no such thing. We was merely talking, that's all.'

'Yeah,' she insisted sarcastically, 'about me, and I'll bet my life you weren't saying anything nice, either!'

'Think what you like,' he said, shrugging his shoulders as he stood up, having washed his hands and face, 'but the fact is there ain't no way you can know for sure what we was talking about, seeing how you don't speak one word of Ute.' He turned away from his scowling sister and started back towards the tepee, wiping his wet hands on his britches. She rose from her kneeling position on the bank of the stream and hurried after him.

'You're right,' she admitted, with a mischievous grin, 'I can't prove nothing, but I still say you was being mean and there's one thing you need to remember, little brother.'

'And what would that be?'

'I always get my own back!' As she said it, she winked and patted him playfully on the shoulder, before taking the lead on the walk back to their temporary lodgings. It left him shaking his head and just a little bit anxious about what she might have in mind. The one thing he had learned from day one was not to underestimate her cunning ways.

By mid-morning, Josie found herself alone with Star and her female relatives, who had all come over to pay their respects. Her pa had gone off hunting with Star's brother and a handful of other warriors, while Hawk had wandered off right after breakfast in search of his cousins, intent on engaging in some game or prank out of sight of the adults. As she was unable to join in with their conversations, boredom soon overtook her, at which point she decided to take a stroll through the peaceful encampment.

She had been strolling along, head down, deep in thought, for several minutes when the sound of children laughing and shouting caught her attention. Without breaking stride, she headed off in the direction of the disturbance, chewing on a long piece of grass she plucked from the ground. When she crested a slight rise on the edge of the village her eyes beheld a wondrous sight. In the wide, grassy hollow below a crowd of thirty or more children of all ages were playing a rather fast and violent game using sticks and a ball of rags.

At first glance there didn't appear to be any proper rules and it was impossible to tell if they were playing in teams or as individuals. Nor could she decide upon the object of the game. The players constantly wrestled their way past one another, occasionally resorting to giving a rival a sharp crack across the shins with their stick if they didn't get out of the way quickly enough. And right in the middle of all the action was her brother, dribbling the ball of rags, dodging blows from other players' sticks, yelling his glee at the top of his lungs.

It was Josie's kind of game, but unfortunately, as she lacked the necessary equipment, she was forced to adopt a watching brief. She sat down, hugging her knees to her chest, wishing she could rush down the slope and join in. There were as many girls playing as boys, and they gave as good as they got. No quarter was asked or given. Having said that, no one seemed to get badly hurt and bruises were quickly forgotten in the quest to get close enough to have a hack at the improvised ball.

She had been watching for several minutes when two burly youths wandered on to the field, carrying a pair of rabbits they had killed while hunting in the woods. They rudely pushed a number of the excited children, who only had eyes for the ball, out of their way. The game came to an abrupt end when the ball rolled to a stop inches from the two stern-faced youths. The taller of the pair shouted something which caused the players to freeze on the spot.

Josie instantly recognized him as the boy who had insulted her on the trail. She also knew him for what he was, the equivalent of the schoolyard bully. She glared at him contemptuously from on high waiting to see if anyone would dare to retrieve the ball. Such a course of action seemed extremely unlikely, given the fact that the truculent youth stood several inches taller and many pounds heavier than any of the boys involved in the game. However, much to her surprise, her brother quickly strode forward to confront the youth.

Hawk stood toe to toe with the haughty young warrior who was intent on spoiling their fun. He spat at his feet prior to hurling a torrent of abuse in his direction. Without a second thought the hunter grabbed hold of Hawk by the front of his shirt and threw him violently to the ground. He followed up with a vicious kick to the ribs.

Josie came to her feet and hurtled down the gentle slope to the rescue with all the speed she could muster. She wove her way through the cordon of intimidated young children, pausing just long enough to indicate to a small boy in the centre of the crowd that she had need of the stick he held in his quivering hands. When he showed no sign of complying with her wishes, Josie unceremoniously yanked it from his hands before continuing on her way to confront the youth who had chosen to throw his weight about.

'You leave my brother alone!' she yelled. The look upon the youth's face as he replied in his own language told Josie all she needed to know. He was insulting her, and for that he would pay, just as he would for hurting her brother. 'Back off, lame brain,' she snarled. 'I know you, and I know you speak English.'

'Go away, little white girl,' hissed the young warrior's equally odious companion. 'Your brother has dared to challenge his elders and betters, and for that he must be punished. And if you get in our way, you will also suffer much pain.'

'Yeah, well we'll see about that, won't we?' she replied, pulling a funny face. Without any warning, she suddenly wielded the stick like a club, cracking it wickedly across the shins of each of the shocked youths in turn. They instantly began to howl with pain and rage as they hopped about on the spot, grabbing hold of their badly-bruised shins with both hands. Before they had a chance to recover from her initial assault, their nemesis followed up by whacking them time and again across their backs and shoulders with her trusty weapon.

Bruised, abused, winded and totally humiliated, the bullies swiftly retreated from the field of battle. Josie went after them, swinging the stick above her head, screaming at the top of her voice like a whirling dervish. She whacked them repeatedly across their exposed backs and rumps, seemingly intent on shattering every bone in their aching bodies, as they tried to make good their escape back into the woods from whence they came.

Loud laughter and great cheering from the delighted children who ran at her side echoed out across the land in response to her every blow. Only when the errant youths finally disappeared into the trees, leaving their freshly-killed game trailing in their wake, did Josie lower her improvised club and call off the chase.

Hawk pushed his way through the milling throng of admirers surrounding his sweating, panting sister to proffer his thanks for her prompt and decisive action. 'You really are something, Josie,' he said with a grin as he rubbed his aching shoulder. 'Those two young bucks never knew what hit them!'

'They had it coming,' she insisted. 'Ain't no one allowed to hit my brother, apart from me, or pa, of course!'

'Oh, I'll never give you cause to hit me ever again, Josie, I surrender,' he said, throwing up his hands, 'after what I just seen I'd rather face a wounded bear than tangle with you. But I reckon it proves one thing you told me.'

'And what would that be, little brother?'

'You do get your own back!'

Josie's running battle with Walks By Night and Young Bear soon became the talk of the village. Her pa got to hear about it even before his proud offspring made it back to the tepee to help pack for their homeward journey. Although he didn't rightly approve of girls fighting, or boys come to that, except when it was strictly necessary, he felt genuine pride in his daughter for the way she had faced up to a tricky situation.

Everyone in the village was delighted to hear that two youths, who had become far too big for their own moccasins, had finally got their come-uppance. The chastened and badly-bruised boys kept well away from the village until they were able to sneak back to their respective family tepees under the cover of darkness. If they imagined for a moment that their misdemeanours would be easily forgotten, they were in for an unpleasant surprise. Their wounded egos received a further battering from angry fathers who felt their sons' actions had brought shame on their families. They were also the butt of many a good joke around the encampment. Tales of their ignominious defeat at the hands of a young white girl were destined to be told around winter campfires for many a year to come.

The fathers of the disgraced youths dropped by the next morning, just as the family were preparing to pull out, to offer their apologies to Josie and Hawk. When her father translated the warriors' glowing tributes to her courage, Josie blushed bright pink and had a devil of a time controlling an inner bout of the giggles. However, the gift they brought to honour her bravery and make amends for their sons' foolishness left her utterly speechless. The pretty yellow colt with its flowing white mane was the stuff of dreams for any young girl. Although words failed her, the pure, unbridled joy and excitement that sang and danced in her wide eyes as she flung her arms around her new mount's neck said it all. The warriors were delighted by her response and returned to their lodges satisfied that family honour had been restored.

12

Curtis McKenzie was a highly contented man. The doubts he had first harboured as to the wisdom of bringing his young eastern-bred, tenderfoot daughter to his home in the mountains had long since melted away with the last of the lingering winter snow. Although her arrival had initially caused some resentment in his son and upheaval in all their lives, they had faced up to their respective difficulties and made the necessary adjustments.

Josie was thriving in her new environment and was growing more accustomed to life in the wilderness with each passing day. She was at peace with herself and Hawk, who she now accepted as her brother as well as an equal. He had taken to her too, and they were now the best of friends and virtually inseparable. That's not to say that they didn't have their moments, but then what two siblings don't?

The children often accompanied their father on his hunting and trapping trips. They helped him set his traps and also took it in turns to take care of routine tasks around their nightly campsite. He also took every opportunity to teach Josie the secrets of the high country, including how to use a gun, skin game, move quietly through the wilderness and how to look for sign. She proved to be a quick and willing learner, relishing every moment they shared together on their various expeditions.

Josie was growing closer to both her father and new stepmother with each passing day. Now, after little more than two months living together in the tiny, cramped cabin in the sheltered valley, they were truly a family. And at the very moment that McKenzie had found inner contentment of a kind he had never previously felt, he had to absent himself from the family he adored. The summer rendezvous was calling. He had a pile of furs to trade and they needed supplies to see them through the next winter.

'How long are you gonna be gone, pa?' asked Josie from the doorway of the cabin as he finished tying a string of beaver pelts to the last of his pack animals.

'Hard to say exactly, Josie,' he replied. 'It'll probably take me four or five days to reach the rendezvous site and the same to get back, but the actual trading can go quick or it can go slow, depending on circumstances I don't rightly want to go into.'

'He means whether they all get drunk or not!' interjected Hawk from over near the barn.

'Hawk! Your father is not a drinking man, you know that,' scolded Star as she came to stand behind

Josie, resting her hands on her amused stepdaughter's shoulders.

'That ain't what his friends all say!' McKenzie pushed his weatherbeaten hat back further on his head and grinned.

'Now don't go believing everything you hear from some dumb mountain man,' he insisted. 'Oh, I'll admit, I like a drink or two when I'm visiting one of the settlements or attending rendezvous, but you'll never see me drunk, boy. A man needs to keep his wits about him at all times, especially at rendezvous. There's many an unscrupulous trader or jealous trapper attending such a powwow who'll try to rob you blind if'n you don't watch out. Alcohol and trading don't mix. No, sir, they never did, and that's a fact you'd do well to remember when you're old enough to take in your own hard-earned furs.'

'I'm old enough now,' rejoined Hawk, strolling across to join his pa in front of the cabin. 'You should take me with you, pa.'

'If he goes, then I go too,' said Josie.

'Neither of you are going, and that's final,' stated McKenzie, firmly as he came forward to kiss his wife goodbye. 'Rendezvous is no place for kids. But don't go fretting none, you'll both get to go, when you grow up a little; maybe in say ten or twelve years.'

'Very funny, pa,' mocked Hawk. McKenzie hugged and kissed Josie and then strode forward to tousle his son's dark hair.

'Look after your ma and Josie for me, Hawk, and

stay close to the house until I return.'

'Sure thing, pa,' replied the youngster, smiling warmly. 'You can count on me.'

With his three heavily-laden pack animals in tow behind him, McKenzie climbed into his saddle and kicked his mount into motion towards the head of the valley. He paused briefly, once he had forded the shallow stream, to give them a final wave before continuing on his way.

Spring was giving way to the pleasant warmth of early summer. The hills and valleys were ablaze with colour, the air, clean, fresh and invigorating. It felt good to be alive as he continued on his unhurried way through the unspoilt, red-rocked country that would lead him steadily down on to the plains at the foot of the Rockies where the annual rendezvous was due to be held. Here, mountain men from hundreds of miles around would come together to trade their furs with the hard-bargaining merchants from the frontier towns, who generally paid them with supplies to see them through the next winter.

After months of lonely solitude in a harsh and unforgiving land, the trappers were also determined to let off steam and have a good time. There was plenty of entertainment on offer: pretty Indian maidens; shooting, wrestling and bare-knuckle contests; horse and running races; tall tales around the campfires; and no shortage of hard liquor. Brutal, no-quarter asked, no-quarter given, drunken fights, fought out over the most trivial of issues with fist, knife and gun, were quite commonplace. A pile of rocks and a simple wooden marker served as a final resting place for any poor soul who was unfortunate enough to overestimate his ability to deal with a rival who refused to back down. In almost every case, the cause of the fight could be traced back to too much liquor or foolish pride.

Late on the third day of his journey, as he splashed his way across a shallow, rippling stream at the entrance to a narrow, wooded draw, he sensed that he was being watched. The prickly feeling at the back of his neck refused to go away as he slowly and surreptitiously surveyed the shadowy terrain through narrowing eyes. He deftly slipped the fingers of his right hand inside his unbuttoned buckskin jacket and rested them loosely against the butt of the pistol he carried in the thick leather belt around his waist.

It was the perfect place for any would-be bushwhacker to tackle a lone rider, for the dense foliage and jagged cliffs could easily have masked an entire army. A bead of sweat formed on his brow as his mount reached the far bank of the stream. Experience told him he would have only a split second in which to react when the attack came.

'Any moment now,' he whispered to himself, as he paralleled the stream at a walk, fully alert and ready to do battle. It was at that precise moment that two men emerged from the cover of the trees off to his left, leading their mounts by the reins. The tension in his body disappeared immediately as he recognized their smiling faces.

'We was all set to plug ya,' revealed Jed Smart on reaching the spot where McKenzie had dismounted to water his horse. 'We thought you was some Ute buck out for our hair.'

'And I thought you were a pair of no-good desperadoes, skulking in the woods, hell bent on relieving me of my hard-earned pelts,' replied a grinning McKenzie, shaking hands with each man in turn. 'How you been, boys?'

'Fine, just fine,' said Joe Maddocks.

'Had any trouble with my Ute friends?'

'Nope,' replied Maddocks with a shake of his head. 'As a matter of fact, we ain't set eyes on another living soul, red or white, since we left your place.'

'I don't reckon there can be any Injuns in these mountains,' interjected Smart, instinctively flexing the leg that remained slightly stiff from the arrow wound he had suffered.

'Oh, they're here all right,' insisted McKenzie with a grin, 'just 'cause you ain't seen 'em, don't mean they ain't around.'

'Well in that case,' said Maddocks, 'if you're heading for rendezvous, I reckon we might just tag along. It might just guarantee we get there in one piece!'

Although McKenzie generally shunned the company of others on the trail, he raised no objection to them riding with him on the last leg of their journey. As the sun was already beginning to slip behind the mountains, they decided to set up camp for the night at the far end of the draw. While Maddocks and Smart saw to the horses and got a fire going, McKenzie headed out into the woods to kill a deer for their supper.

It was while they were filling their bellies with succulent char-broiled venison steaks that McKenzie alerted his companions to his secondary purpose in attending the annual gathering on the plains. He was hoping that during the trading or the nightly drinking sessions some loose-tongued individual would let slip some information about the raid on the peaceful Ute camp. It was the main reason he had opted to trade his furs at the rendezvous rather than make the slightly shorter trek into Santa Fe that he normally favoured.

'So you've a hankering to avenge your red friends?' remarked Maddocks, wiping steak juice from his mouth before it could dribble into his beard. McKenzie merely nodded as he lit himself a smoke. 'Could be a mighty dangerous undertaking.'

'I reckon so,' replied McKenzie, 'but it needs doing.'

'Ain' many going to get themselves too upset over a few dead Utes,' interjected Smart. 'If'n you go poking around too much, like as not you'll end up with a knife stuck in your ribs.' McKenzie shrugged his shoulders.

'This is something I have to do.'

'Then it's just as well that you'll have us around to watch your back,' said Smart, grinning like a bear who'd just found a tree stump full of honey. 'I reckon I owe 'em for that arrow I took in the leg, and if there's one thing me and ole Joe love it's a good fight!'

13

They arrived at the rendezvous just before noon the following day. The tented encampment and improvised trade centre made for a colourful and impressive spectacle, stretching for more than a mile down the grassy, western bank of the Clear Butte River. Several hundred mountain men – mostly seasoned veterans, with just a sprinkling of younger men who had managed to safely negotiate their first winter in the wilderness – were already in residence, together with various small bands of Indians, who kept their distance from one another to prevent old tribal disputes getting in the way of the trading. While the vast majority of the trappers came to replenish exhausted supplies and damaged equipment, the Indians were mainly interested in obtaining whiskey, tobacco and guns, although those who had few furs to trade were always forced to settle for colourful cloth for their womenfolk, or bags of sugar or flour.

The bartering and impromptu entertainment was

already in full swing when they rode in. 'So, do we trade first and ask questions later?' asked Smart, standing tall in the saddle to see if he could spot any familiar faces amongst the seething crowd of stinking frontiersmen. Having stretched weary limbs, he eased himself down into the saddle once more.

'That would seem to be the best bet,' agreed McKenzie. 'Our nosing around will attract less attention when folks begin to get liquored up after dark.'

'Then let's go see what these furs'll fetch,' said Maddocks, reaching out to pat the huge bundle of shiny beaver pelts strapped to the back of the cantankerous mule at his side. 'Once we've got this little load off of our hands, I'm of a mind to get washed on the outside and wet on the inside before we go poking around for trouble. If'n I'm gonna get myself shot, I figure on having a little fun first!'

It was late in the afternoon by the time they off-loaded their merchandise. The merchants, as always, drove a hard bargain, but they all felt reasonably happy with the goods they got in exchange for the sweat of their labours. The furs, which were destined to be turned into the hats which were all the fashion in Europe, were promptly thrown on top of the ever-growing pile that threatened to break the long trestle tables in front of the merchants' wagons.

Having stowed their new gear and supplies, they wandered off to join the crowd that had gathered just outside the temporary settlement to watch and wager on the horse-racing that was in progress. Maddocks took a particular fancy to a frisky palomino pony ridden by a young half-breed, sporting a black top-hat complemented by an eagle feather. Smart warned him that he would be wasting his money, but his companion insisted on wagering a dollar, which he promptly lost when the horse and rider in question finished next to last! When he had finally finished cussing and kicking the ground in exasperation, he allowed his friends to lead him away in search of a consoling drink, a hot meal and the bath he had been promising himself for weeks.

Having accomplished all three things by the time the sun set behind the western mountains, they led their horses and mules off in search of a suitable spot to bed down for the night. They found room amongst a handful of fellow trappers in a small grove of cottonwoods down by the river. In spite of their promise to remain sober, both Smart and Maddocks were much the worse for drink. It meant that McKenzie had to leave them behind to guard their possessions while he strolled through the noisy encampment in search of any information.

As he wandered quietly and unobtrusively from campfire to campfire, keeping his ear close to the ground, he had to dodge the occasional drunk who staggered unapologetically into his path. The occasional gunshot or raised voice caused him to alter course and investigate, but they all proved to be dead ends.

As the night wore on he grew increasingly tired of

listening in the shadows to all the hot air and inane ragging emanating from the mouths of his fellow mountain men. True, a few of the stories they brought vividly to life for their audiences were quite funny, but that's all they were, stories, which had little or no basis in fact. When he overheard a young army deserter turned mule-skinner claiming that the South was winning the war of cessation from the Union, he decided he had had enough for one night.

He was on his way back to join Maddocks and Smart, intent on catching some much needed shut-eye, when he encountered two young trappers leaving the tented saloon close to the centre of the camp. His eyes immediately fell on the dark, shiny trophy carried by the shorter of the pair. It halted him dead in his tracks.

'See, I told you they'd laugh at us when you asked for a beer, Johnny,' said the taller, darker youth, moodily. 'I told you they'd say you was too young. It was just a waste of time.'

' 'Twern't nothing to do with my age,' snapped the sassy, self-opinionated youth called Johnny, toying irritably with the braided scalp tied to his belt, ' 'twas your Indian blood, Luke Dawson, and you knows it. They didn't want to serve no lousy half-breed!' Dawson instantly grabbed hold of his friend roughly by the sleeve of his jacket with one hand while the other fell to the knife sheaved at his hip.

'I should cut you for that!' he hissed.

'My brother might have something to say about

that,' warned his mouthy friend, pulling himself free of the iron grip on his arm. 'In fact, I reckon he might just kill ya if he knew you'd laid hands on me.'

'Where'd you get the scalp lock on your belt, boy?' McKenzie's unexpected question and towering presence directly in front of them caused the squabbling friends to stop dead in their tracks.

'That ain't none of your business, friend,' sneered the one called Johnny.

'I'm making it my business, and I ain't your friend,' insisted McKenzie.

'Get out of my way, stranger.' The kid tried to sidestep around the trapper, but McKenzie swiftly countered his move, just as he did a second attempt to get past him. 'It looks to me like you're looking for trouble, mister.'

'It do?'

'Yeah, it do.'

'Tell me what I want to know, bub, then maybe there won't be no trouble. Now, I'll ask you just one more time, where'd ya get the hair?'

'My name ain't bub, it's Johnny, Johnny Hampson,' snarled the youngster, in a manner which suggested it should mean something to the stubborn man obstructing his path.

'I don't care if your name's Abraham Lincoln, you'll answer the question.'

'The hell I will!' yelled Johnny Hampson, his hand falling to the pistol on his hip. Before he cold draw his weapon, McKenzie stepped forward to stun him with a full-blooded punch to the side of the jaw. The kid toppled over backwards with a loud grunt and landed in an ungainly, motionless heap on the muddy ground. McKenzie's own navy Colt appeared in his as if by magic, when the second youth's dark eyes suggested that he was about to try to avenge his fallen companion.

'Don't even think about it!' warned McKenzie, slowly moving his gun from side to side. 'You as much as move a muscle without my say so and I'll shoot you down like a mangey cur. Now, real slow and easy, drop your gun and knife on the ground in front of you.' The cold, implacable stare that accompanied his harshly-spoken words convinced the frightened youth that the mountain man wasn't bluffing, so he simply nodded and obeyed. 'Now I want answers, and if I even suspect you're lying, then you're a dead man, understand?' The colour drained from the young half-breed's face as he nodded again.

'What do you want to know?' he asked.

'Where'd your friend get the scalp?'

'It was a present from his big brother, Mike.'

'How'd he come by it?' pressed McKenzie.

The youth suddenly looked deathly afraid. He swallowed hard, shuffled his moccasined feet uncomfortably and then trembled in spite of his grim determination to remain calm. 'If I tell you, you'll probably kill me.'

'Could be,' agreed McKenzie, cocking the hammer of the heavy Colt in his hand to show that he meant business, 'but try holding out on me and you won't even get time to say your prayers, and that's a promise, son.' Luke Dawson let out a lingering sigh.

'OK,' he said, 'I'll tell you what you want to know.'

The mountain man kept his gun pointed at the young renegade's chest as he listened patiently to his sorry tale. What he heard made his blood boil. Just as he had suspected all along, the youths were members of a gang of frontier low-life who preyed on honest men. They had ridden up into the mountains in early spring, under the leadership of Johnny Hampson's elder brother Mike, intent upon relieving unwary, lonely trappers of their hard-won furs. Despite the promise of rich, easy pickings, they had little to show for their nefarious activities until the moment they tumbled upon the peaceful Ute camp.

Dawson insisted that neither he nor his unconscious friend had taken any active part in the blood-letting. Their four companions had left them guarding the horses while they snuck into the camp and butchered the sleeping Indians at close quarters. The killers had then scalped and mutilated the dead before looting the camp. It was the scalp Mike Hampson had handed to his kid brother as a grisly keepsake of the raid that had first caught McKenzie's attention when their paths had crossed.

'So you didn't kill any Utes?' scoffed the mountain man. Dawson shook his head. 'And you expect me to believe that?'

'It's the truth,' insisted the youth, desperately. 'It

was all Mike's doing, honest.'

'But you shared in the plunder?' Dawson nodded. Fear shone in his dark eyes. His captor's cold implacable eyes stared deep into his very soul. He was convinced the trapper was going to kill him where he stood.

'I've done some awful things in my life, mister,' he confessed, 'but I ain't ever killed no Injuns or shot a man in the back.'

'You're running with a bad crowd son, and it can only end one way.'

'You're gonna kill me ain't you?'

'I'm thinking on it,' admitted McKenzie, evenly. 'Like as not if I don't, some other fella will, or you'll end up swinging from the end of a rope.'

'I'll ride out right now, I'll quit the Hampsons' and mend my ways. I swear I'll try to find honest work, if'n you'll just let me go, mister.'

'Where can I find Mike Hampson?' demanded a stern-faced McKenzie.

Dawson knew he was stuck between a rock and a hard place. He quickly thought things over. 'Why should I tell you? You're going to kill me anyway.'

'You have precisely five seconds to tell me what I want to know,' said McKenzie, 'before I put a bullet through your right kneecap. And if that fails to loosen your tongue, then the next one will go through your left. You'll never walk again.'

Dawson knew he wasn't bluffing. As if to emphasize the point, McKenzie pointed the barrel of his pistol directly at the youth's right leg. Sweat began to trickle down his captive's forehead. He didn't want to carry out his threat, for the sound of gunfire might bring unwanted company and awkward questions. Sudden, spontaneous violence was no stranger to the annual rendezvous. The odd drunken quarrel or long-standing dispute had always been settled with fist or knife or gun. But such bitter confrontations also invariably drew a crowd of interested bystanders, like a moth to a flame. He wanted to avoid such a scene, if at all possible.

'The last we saw of Mike and the others, they was heading for Frenchie La Mare's saloon down by the river,' said Dawson, trying to control a bout of the shakes.

'How will I recognize him?'

'You won't have any problem spotting Mike Hampson in a crowd. He's kinda short and wiry, and he wears a coonskin hat with two black and white eagle feathers at the top of the tail. He's also got a jagged scar on his left cheek, the legacy of a knife fight with a river-boat gambler few years back.'

'And what about the others with him?'

'Ben Peters is around six foot tall, and wears a patch over his left eye. Jake Plummer and Frank Jasper are both fairly short, stocky and bearded. Plummer carries a Bowie knife in his belt and has rotted teeth, while Jasper walks with a slight limp, on account of an arthritic knee, and never goes anywhere without his old-fashioned flintlock rifle.'

McKenzie carefully released the hammer of his Colt before stowing the weapon back in his belt. 'Leave your weapons where they are and make yourself scarce, kid,' he said. 'And if'n you try to warn your friends, I'll find you for sure, and kill you without a second thought.'

'I won't say nothin',' insisted Dawson, spreading his hands wide to indicate that he wanted no further trouble. 'You have my word on it.'

'Be on you way then, and don't look back.'

'What about Johnny? He's still out cold.' McKenzie raised his eyebrows, and then stepped forward to kick the prone body of Johnny Hampson viciously in the ribs, to make sure he wasn't faking it. The youngster made no sound.

'I don't reckon he'll be causing any more trouble for a while,' said McKenzie. 'Now get going, before I change my mind.'

Dawson took off into the darkness half-expecting a bullet in the back. When it never came, he counted his blessings and kept going, totally oblivious to the fact that the mountain man was dogging his every step to ensure that he made good on his promise to quit the camp. Only when he had collected his horse and possessions and set off down the moonlit trail in the direction of Santa Fe did McKenzie turn back.

He found his two friends snoring loudly by the fire they had lit to keep the pesky biting insects at bay. Before waking them, he opted to brew some strong black coffee to help clear their senses for the task which lay ahead. Although they were initially rather unhappy about being wakened from their peaceful, dream-filled slumbers, McKenzie's news, coupled with the steaming coffee, immediately had the desired effect on their weary, whiskey-dulled bodies.

'How do you want to play this hand out, pard?' asked Maddocks, pouring himself a second cup of coffee from the enamel pot simmering over the fire.

'Well, there's four of them, not counting the kid I've disabled some, and they're meaner than a pack of wolves. If'n we're gonna take 'em, we need to do it quick and head on before they know what's hit them.'

'An ambush in the mountains might be more appropriate for the likes of them,' said Smart, emptying the dregs from his tin cup before reaching for a refill.

'No,' stated Maddocks, firmly, 'shooting a man in the back don't sit well with me, not even one like Mike Hampson.'

'I agree,' said McKenzie. 'I intend to face them out. I want them to look death in the face before I send them to hell. But I'll understand if you fellas don't want any part of this.'

'Jest try keeping us out of it!' exclaimed Smart. 'Then you really will have a parcel of trouble on your hands.'

Once he was certain his companions had fully sobered up, McKenzie led them away in the direction of Frenchie La Mare's saloon. A bright yellow, shimmering moon cast an eerie glow on to the encampment from out of the inky blue, star-spangled sky as they drew closer to the river and the sound of music and laughter. With any luck, the men they were after would be too liquored up to offer much in the way of resistance.

The saloon was still packed with late-night revellers. The smoky interior made it difficult to see anything clearly, but as their eyes adjusted to the hazy atmosphere, they saw that every seat was taken and that there was hardly elbow room at the bar. Most of the well-oiled trappers were swapping stories with old friends, a few were losing their money at the gambling tables while others were staggering about the dance floor wrapped around one of Frenchie's pretty young camp followers.

'I don't see them,' advised McKenzie as he led his companions towards the bar. 'Let's see if Frenchie knows them.'

Frenchie La Mare was a bald-headed, truly colourful, larger-than-life character who possessed the loudest, most raucous belly laugh anywhere in the west. His squat frame and enormous, heavy girth would have provided a considerable challenge for the stoutest horse, had he ever chosen to ride anything other than a wagon.

He owned a flourishing trading post down on the Fancy River, fifty miles north of Santa Fe, which provided him with a good income. The profits he gleaned from the pockets of the mountain men who attended the annual gathering at the foot of the

Rocky Mountains was a welcome bonus, but he came as much for the conversation and the chance to revisit his youth as he did for the money and furs. Although he had a pleasant disposition, La Mare refused to suffer fools gladly and his formidable bulk and strength ensured that he was treated with the greatest respect by friend and foe alike. He was certainly not a man to be trifled with. McKenzie had only met him once, but he knew him to be an honest rogue who would take a dim view of what Hampson and his cronies had done.

'What'll it be, friend?' asked Frenchie when McKenzie finally managed to reach the bar and catch the man's eye.

'Some information,' replied McKenzie.

'I sell beer and hard liquor, not information,' said La Mare, firmly.

'I think you'll want to help when you know what this is all about,' insisted McKenzie.

'OK,' agreed La Mare. 'But make it quick, I've other customers waiting.'

McKenzie told him the whole story, at which point the saloon keeper advised him that he did indeed know the men he was after, and that he didn't have much time for them. La Mare went on to explain that other trappers tended to keep well clear of them because of their reputation for causing trouble. They had spent most of the night drinking at a table close to the bar, but had left the tent some fifteen minutes before Curtis McKenzie arrived, within moments of

Hampson's kid brother showing up looking much the worse for wear.

'I think I know where they're camped,' said McKenzie.

'Are you right sure you want to go there?' queried La Mare. 'Them guys are meaner than a cornered grizzly.'

'I know,' said McKenzie, 'but this is something I have to do.'

'Well, good luck, friend,' said La Mare pleasantly as McKenzie made for the exit.

The renegades were long gone by the time McKenzie and his companions closed in on their camp site.

'Judging by the direction of their tracks, I'd say they was heading back up into the mountains,' observed Maddocks, as he stood up again having gone down on his haunches to examine the sign they had left behind.

'Seems most likely,' agreed Smart. 'So what do we do now?'

'Well I don't know about you two,' said McKenzie, 'but I aim to catch some sleep, and then, come first light, I'm heading out after them.'

'Then I guess we'll be a-going with ya,' stated Maddocks. 'Never did believe in leaving a job unfinished.'

14

Throughout the bright, warm morning the vengeful trappers relentlessly trailed their quarry up into the mountains. The tracks of five riders led them due west towards Ute country. McKenzie harboured no doubts that the killers expected them to follow. He figured that they would either try to outrun them or choose a likely spot to spring an ambush. When he shared his thoughts with his companions, they decided to fan out so as not to present an easy target for any would-be bushwhacker. Narrow passes and wooded hillsides were treated with grave suspicion as they rode on with senses on full alert.

At midday they stopped beside a clear, babbling stream to rest their tiring mounts. They had pressed on as quickly as they dared, given the need to preserve the strength of their mounts, but were still several hours behind the renegades. McKenzie kept watch over the grazing horses and mules while his companions boiled some coffee to wash down the beef jerky they had packed for their journey.

'We'll keep the bacon and beans for when we camp tonight,' said Maddocks, handing McKenzie a cup of sweet black coffee and strip of dried meat. McKenzie nodded his thanks. 'You still figure they mean to jump us?'

'Yeah. It's what I'd do in their position.'

'Well I think you've called it wrong,' said Smart, wandering over to join them on the banks of the crystal clear stream. 'If'n you ask me, they're intent on putting as much distance as possible between them and us. We've already ridden past many a likely spot for an ambush, so I reckon they'd have tried something by now if they was of a mind to.'

'Maybe,' conceded McKenzie. 'But we'd best keep our wits about us all the same.'

All through the long, hot afternoon, they remained ever watchful. As the sun slipped behind the mountains, they entered a wide valley with steep, densely wooded sides. It seemed as good a spot as any to spend the night. After seeing to their mounts, they set up camp in the shelter of a large boulder on the bank of the shallow river that flowed through the valley.

'Clean mountain air, the company of good friends and a plate of bacon and beans, it don't get any better than this,' said Smart as he accepted a plate full of hot food from Maddocks, whose turn it was to cook.

'No it don't,' agreed his friend, happily. 'And I tell you what, I never get tired of gazing up at a sky full of stars. Makes a fella certain there really is a God.'

'I'll stand the first watch,' offered McKenzie as he washed his plate in the river, having finished his meal. He collected his rifle from beside his bedroll and moved off towards the grazing animals to the accompaniment of the mournful howl of a lone coyote somewhere far off in the darkness.

'Wake me in a couple of hours,' Smart called after him, having swallowed a mouthful of beans, 'and I'll spell ya.'

After an uneventful night, they were back in the saddle as the first grey light of dawn was registering in the eastern sky. By making such an early start, they hoped to close the gap on Mike Hampson and his band of cold-hearted killers. McKenzie judged that the renegades were probably no more than two or three hours ahead of them. He was also beginning to think that Jed Smart was right about them being intent on getting away rather than fighting it out. But with any luck, they would catch up with them by nightfall.

Late in the morning they began to ascend a narrow, winding trail that clung perilously to the steep sides of a towering, snow-peaked mountain. They rode in single file, maintaining maximum concentration, as they snaked their way up and round the mountain, for one mistake would have seen them tumble into the rocky gorge and fast-flowing river far below. Smart took the lead with Maddocks right behind him and McKenzie bringing up the rear.

Their mounts were experienced in dealing with

such terrain and showed no fear. McKenzie felt ill at ease, for there was little or no cover on the trail should they come under attack. If he himself had been planning an ambush, he would most certainly have taken advantage of the possibilities offered by rugged terrain. The thought had no sooner entered his head than gunfire erupted from the far side of the narrow gorge as they rounded a sharp bend, halfway up the mountain. With no shelter of any kind, no room in which to manoeuvre and nowhere to run, they were sitting ducks. They never stood a chance.

Smart was the first to fall. His hands went to his chest as a slug knocked him out of the saddle. He never heard Maddocks' warning shout of, 'Ambush!' as he fell into the gorge. His startled cry echoed through the mountains as he bounced off the rocks all the way down to the river's edge, where his lifeless body came to rest up against a round boulder.

With lot lead pinging off the rocks all about him, Maddocks' horse did a half-turn and then reared up in fright. As he fought to control the skittish animal, two bullets slammed into his exposed back. He was dead before he hit the ground.

McKenzie's right hand had just made contact with the rifle at his side when his horse suddenly whinnied and buckled beneath him. As he rolled clear of his dying mount a bullet clipped the side of his head and everything went black.

'We got 'em all!' exclaimed an excited voice. A smiling Johnny Hampson stepped out from behind a pine tree on the far side of the gorge. 'Just like you said we would, Mike.'

'Keep down you, derned fool!' cried his brother anxiously, from where he skulked behind a large rock. 'They might not be dead yet.' The younger Hampson immediately ducked back out of sight. 'What do you reckon, Ben? You see any sign of movement?'

'Naw,' came the reply from further up the gorge. 'We got the job done, fer sure.' One by one the five members of Mike Hampson's gang slowly emerged from cover to survey the scene on the far side of the gorge. The eerie silence was punctuated by Johnny Hampson's demonic laughter ringing through the still air.

'See what happens to those who mess with the Hampsons, tough guy!' he yelled at the top of his voice.

'He can't hear you, kid,' said Ben Peters, adjusting his eye-patch, 'he's dead.'

'I don't care,' growled the younger Hampson.

'You sure that one of them was Curtis McKenzie, Frank?' queried Mike Hampson.

Frank Jasper nodded, spat out a chaw of tobacco and then said, 'Yeah, I'm sure. I had a run-in with him a few years back when I was in Santa Fe, and I never forget a face or a name.'

'They say he's got a cabin up in Ute country, and a pretty young squaw and a kid,' said Ben Peters.

'Let's go,' said Mike Hampson, grinning broadly. He turned on his heels and began to carefully scale the rocky mountainside at their backs. 'I reckon we should pay our respects to his widow; it seems like the very least we can do.'

15

Star was down by the stream fetching water when she spotted riders off in the distance. At first she thought it must be Hawk and Josie returning from their morning's hunting trip. They were running low on fresh meat so she had allowed the children to try to scare up a couple of rabbits or a small deer to see them through until her husband's return. She set her bucket down between her feet and shielded her eyes against the bright glare of the sun as she gazed towards the approaching riders in an attempt to identify them. As they drew closer she counted five and assumed it must be Curtis and some old friends back from the rendezvous. Without a second thought she hurried back to the house, bucket in hand, to prepare a welcoming meal.

By the time she had the stove lit, the horses were cantering up to the cabin. She gave the remains of the venison stew a final stir and then went to the door to greet her husband and his guests. The smile on her face vanished in a trice when she stepped outside and found herself confronted by five menacing-looking strangers.

'You must be McKenzie's wife,' growled the man in the centre. Star's nervous eyes settled on the vivid scar on his left cheek as she nodded. The old wound served to accentuate his rough and generally unpleasant appearance and demeanour.

'Who are you?' she asked, her eyes moving along the line of motionless, unsmiling riders. 'What do you want here?'

'You might say we're old friends of your husband's, little lady,' replied Mike Hampson. His companions chuckled. 'He told us to be sure and stop by any time we was passing.'

'My husband's not here.'

'Yeah, we know. But that don't mean you can't be sociable to his friends, now does it? I'm sure you can spare a little food for me and my companions.'

'I have some stew warming on the stove,' she offered, recognizing the danger she was in and trying to buy time. She knew instinctively that they were bad men, but alone and unarmed she stood no chance of fighting them off. At least if she got them seated at the table inside the cabin, she might somehow be able to get hold of the rifle hanging over the fireplace or find some way of slipping out and making a run for it. It was her only real hope, but she would have to make her move quickly, for the children could return at any time. 'Come on in.'

The five men promptly dismounted and followed

her inside the cabin. They sat down at the table as she moved towards the stove to see if the stew was ready. Having given it another stir, she collected plates and cutlery and set the table. As she swayed past the man wearing an eye-patch he grabbed hold of her roughly by the arm, causing her to squeal out in alarm.

'Maybe you and I can have a little fun after I've eaten,' he sneered. 'You sure are a pretty little thing for a Ute squaw, and I bet you know how to make a man like me real happy.'

Without a second thought, Star picked up the knife she had just placed before him and plunged it into his right hand, pinning it to the table. He instantly let go of her arm, howling in pain and rage. She ran to the fireplace, only to be cut down by two bullets in the back as she reached up to grab the rifle hanging above the mantlepiece.

'What did you go and do that for?' roared Mike Hampson, angrily. 'She ain't gonna pleasure us none now, is she?'

'I had to do it,' argued Frank Jasper, lowering his still smoking pistol. 'There's no tellin' what might have happened if she'd got hold of the rifle.'

'You didn't have to kill her,' insisted a frustrated Mike Hampson.

'Never mind her, what about me?' said Ben Peters, gritting his teeth. The excruciating pain that wracked his mutilated hand brought tears to his eyes. 'I need doctoring.'

Mike Hampson moved to his side, held his friend's wrist down on the table and swiftly pulled the knife from his hand. Peters let out a mighty yell and grabbed hold of his wounded limb with his other hand in a vain attempt to stem the flow of blood.

'Find something we can use for a bandage,' instructed Hampson to his kid brother.

'Why me?' he argued.

' 'Cause I said so – now move it.' He sat on the edge of the table. 'That must hurt some.'

'Yeah, it does,' snarled Peters, gripping the back of his hand even tighter.

'We'll patch you up and then ride,' said Hampson. 'We'll take anything that'll be of use to us and then fire the cabin.'

Hawk and Josie were in the woods, a mile to the north of the cabin when the sound of gunfire carried to them on the light breeze. They reined in and looked at each other with puzzled expressions on their faces.

'Sounds like trouble at home,' said Hawk, turning his mount about. 'Let's go.'

By the time they reached the foot of the densely wooded slope, bright red and yellow flames were lacking their way skywards through the pall of black smoke hanging above the distant cabin. A look of horror formed on Hawk's face as he took it all in. Without a second thought he kicked his mount into a flat out gallop towards home. Josie wasted no time in going after him.

They had covered less than a quarter of a mile

when Hawk suddenly reined in. Five mounted men were riding towards them from the direction of the burning cabin. He instinctively knew that their presence spelt danger.

'Quick!' he yelled. 'They're riding after us.'

'But what about Ma?'

'There's nothing we can do for her right now,' insisted her brother. 'Just do like I say.' Josie nodded. 'Follow me, and stay close,' he instructed, as they wheeled their eager mounts about and made a dash for the wooded slope to the rear. 'We'll try to lose them in the woods and double back when it's safe.'

Hawk felt exhilarated, but more than a trifle scared, too. Although he was truly in his element, for he knew the country like the back of his hand, and was also well-versed in how to hide from an enemy, this was not like the fun games he had played with his pa and Ute cousins. The men who were hot on their tail were real bad *hombres*. There was no telling what they would do if they managed to catch up with them. His pa had done much to prepare him for just such an eventuality, now he had to put his knowledge and skills to the ultimate test. He had to pit his wits against five grown men.

He led the way up the steep, narrow trail towards the summit of the hill. Here he turned west along the wooded ridge for several hundred yards before dropping down the far side of the hill. Their Indian ponies made light work of the tricky terrain as they carefully wove their way through the trees towards the sound of a gurgling stream. On reaching it, they waded downstream through the grey, white-capped, rushing waters, until they encountered a low rocky bank, where Hawk chose to return to firm ground.

'Keep to the flat rocks,' he instructed, 'they won't be able to track us here.'

When the rocks gave way to soft ground, he led the way back into the trees on a course that paralleled the ridge high above. They rode on for a mile before coming to rest beneath a rocky ledge. The children dismounted and squatted down close together on the ground. Josie swallowed hard. She looked scared, but said nothing. Hawk gazed nervously all about him while listening intently for any sound for pursuit, but none was forthcoming.

'I reckon we've lost 'em for now,' he said, keeping his voice low.

'Who are they?' whispered Josie.

'I ain't sure,' replied her brother, 'but they're more than likely the same ones who raided the Ute camp.'

'What about Ma?' Hawk shook his head as tears welled up in his sad eyes. He knew with a stone-cold certainty that his mother was dead, but he could not allow his young heart to grieve, not yet, for if he did, he would not be able to think straight, and only a cool, clear head could keep them safe.

'I reckon they've killed Ma,' he announced, fighting back an urge to cry. His sister put a hand to her mouth to suppress her startled cry. 'We'll find out for sure when we get home. But don't worry, Josie, we'll make out OK.' She threw her arms around his neck and clung on tight as tears began to trickle down her face.

'They'll find us, won't they?' she said, resting her head against his shoulder. He gently released himself from her embrace.

'Not until I want them to,' he replied. Josie looked genuinely puzzled.

'What do you mean?'

'I have a plan,' he revealed, as they stood up. Josie turned white as a sheet when he told her what he had in mind.

'We can't,' she argued, 'it's far too dangerous.'

'We don't have a choice,' he insisted. 'We can't let them get away with what they've done. I don't know why they came to our valley, but their type don't give up easily, and if we merely hide out, they'll probably find us in the end.' Doubt still registered in her watery eyes. 'You have to trust me, Josie. You might be older than me, but when it comes to surviving or hunting, I know what I'm doing. We can do this.' Josie wasn't happy, but she knew she had no option but to go along with his daring plan.

'OK,' she said, as they remounted, 'but I don't like it.'

16

Hawk was out of the saddle before his mount came to a standstill in front of the burnt-out shell of the cabin. Tears welled up in his eyes as he went down on his haunches to study sign round about.

'Maybe she got away before they set fire to the cabin,' said Josie. He shook his head.

'Mom's dead,' he sighed. 'And now them that done it have to pay. Let's get to it.'

She knew what he was going through, for she still felt the pain of her own mom's death – despite the passage of time. Now she had lost the love of the patient, caring woman who had willingly stepped into the breach, despite Josie's initial hostility. She followed him towards what remained of the barn, where he retrieved a number of his pa's evil-looking traps from the dying embers of the fire.

'Time to ride,' he said. 'The hunter is about to become the hunted.'

They rode at a gallop towards the forested slopes

due east of their charred home. Once under the cover of the trees they turned north in the direction of the isolated valley where Hawk knew every rock and tree. It was here that he had decided to play out their highly dangerous game of cat and mouse with the killers.

Josie felt deathly afraid. She didn't see how his audacious scheme could possibly work, but she had no choice other than to trust in her brother's instincts for survival. He insisted that if they simply tried to hide, the renegades would eventually run them to ground. It was only a question of time before they returned to the cabin and picked up their trail. Their only chance lay in carrying the fight to their enemy, for it was the last thing they would expect.

Hawk did his level best to confuse their pursuers. He used every trick in the book to mask their trail, including riding through streams and over rocky ledges. Although they never caught sight of another human soul, a sixth sense told him the renegades were right on their tail. Everything was going according to plan.

At dusk they reined in and dismounted in the entrance to a small cave. Having seen to their mounts, the children ate some of the dry rations left over from lunch. It was then, as darkness fell, that Hawk made his move.

'It's time for me to put the next part of the plan into action,' he said, coming to his feet, bow in hand. 'Wait here and watch the horses.'

'No way!' exclaimed Josie, jumping up. 'I'm going with you.'

'No you're not,' corrected Hawk, putting his bow across his shoulder. 'I can move quicker and quieter without you.'

'You can't leave me, I'm scared,' she argued.

'So am I,' he revealed, collecting the beaver traps he had rescued from the barn. 'But I'll be even more scared if I have to look out for you too. This is a one-man raid, Josie, you'd just get in the way. I need to strike quickly and get away in the confusion.'

'What if you get caught?'

'I won't.'

'But what if you do?' He sighed.

'If I'm not back in an hour, take both horses on up the valley. Grey Bull's camped somewhere on the other side of the mountain. His warriors are bound to find you come morning. Just tell him what's happened. He'll know what to do.'

She could tell there was no point in prolonging the debate, so she sat down on a nearby boulder with a sigh. 'Just be real careful,' she implored as he slipped away into the night.

It didn't take him long to locate his quarry. He found them camped by the river a mile to the south of the cave. From his slightly elevated position on the far bank of the wide, shallow river, he could just make out the silhouettes of a number of men seated around a smokeless fire. He considered the possibility of sneaking into the camp to cut loose their horses, but then he remembered what had happened the last time he'd tried such a stunt and decided against it. No, he would keep to his original plan. As long as his nerve didn't fail him at the vital moment, he would make out fine.

Taking great care not to tread on any loose twigs or rocks, he made his way down the wooded slope in the direction of the river. The sound of the mens' relaxed conversation and low laughter carried to him on the breeze as he knelt behind a bush close to the waters edge. He lay his bow and quiver of arrows on the ground, took a deep breath and then waded out into the river carrying his pa's traps in his hands. Although the moon was hidden by clouds, it would only take one careless slip on his part to give the game away, so he was careful not to make any sound as he neared the far bank. As quickly as possible he set his traps in the gently rippling water and then beat a hasty retreat to recover his bow.

The night remained still and quiet, save for the idle chatter of the men gathered about the fireside. It was time to announce his presence. With luck, he might just manage to reduce the odds facing him. He would certainly give them something to think about. Then, come morning, he would ride to Grey Bull's camp with his sister and enlist his Ute relatives help in finishing what he had started.

He took a deep breath to steady his nerves as he notched an arrow to his bowstring. The men lay well within bow range, but it also meant that they could return fire once he launched his silent attack. Of course, they would not be able to locate his exact position in the darkness, and that gave him every chance of escaping in the confusion.

He drew back his bow, took careful aim at a dark shape seated by the fire, and released his first arrow. An awful scream instantly echoed through the hills as the arrow hit its intended target. Gunfire exploded from the other side of the river as someone kicked out the fire to kill the renegades' silhouettes. Having sent two more arrows swishing through the darkness in the general direction of the camp, he took to his heels.

He was halfway up the wooded slope when he heard an agonized scream erupt from the direction of the river. A satisfied grin flickered momentarily across his face. One of the men had evidently stepped in one of the traps he had hidden in the shallow water. It meant that at the very least he had succeeded in wounding two of the gang. Not a bad night's work he thought to himself as he made his way back to join his sister.

He found her sitting on a rock in the mouth of the cave. She jumped to her feet and came to meet him. The gunfire down below had convinced her that he had been killed. 'I thought they'd got you for sure,' she said, patting him on the shoulder.

'No chance,' he retorted.

'So what do we do now?'

'We try to catch a couple of hours' sleep and then

ride to Grey Bull's camp. We can't finish this on our own.'

'But is it safe to stay here?' she queried.

'Yeah,' he replied. 'There's no way they can find this place in the dark. But we'll leave before dawn, just to be sure.' With that, he led her into the cave.

The children were awake and on the move an hour before dawn. By sun-up they had put several miles between themselves and the spot where Hawk had launched his audacious attack. Despite her brother's assurances that they had nothing to fear, Josie remained ill at ease. Her eyes constantly darted every which way for any sign of trouble.

'Why are you so jittery?' demanded Hawk as they crested a low hill and began to descend into a narrow, thickly-wooded gully. 'They ain't gonna catch us now.'

'I'm not so sure about that,' said Josie. 'I've got a bad feeling.'

'Relax,' he insisted, 'we're not far from Grey Bull's camp, everything's gonna work out just fine.'

No sooner were the words out of his mouth than four riders charged out of the woods on either side to surround them. The barrel of a long rifle thudded into the side of Hawk's head as he reached for the bow slung over his shoulder, toppling him from his horse. Josie emitted a high-pitched scream of alarm as she fought to control her prancing mount. One of the encircling riders made a grab for her reins to bring the yellow colt under control.

'Stay put!' barked the man when Josie made to

dismount and go to her brother's aid. He withdrew the wicked-looking Bowie knife from his belt. 'I'll happily slit your throat if you make any more sudden moves.'

'I want to help my brother!' she snapped. 'He's hurt.'

'Not as much as he's gonna be,' said the man who had knocked him from his horse. 'The pair of you are gonna pay for what you and your pa did to me and my friends.'

'What did we ever do to you?' cried Josie.

'Your pa meddled in business that was none of his concern,' he said, 'and then that little half-breed down there went and put an arrow through my kid brother's neck. He died in my arms, and now I aim to skin your brother alive.'

'I want a piece of him too, Mike,' insisted the rider at his side. 'My leg's messed up real bad on account of him. I might never walk right again.'

'I reckon I don't mind sharing him with you, Frank,' agreed Mike Hampson, with a grin. 'As long as I get first licks.'

'But what about what you did to us?' wailed Josie, desperately. 'You killed our ma and burnt our cabin.'

'She had it coming,' sneered the man at her back, who wore his right hand in a sling. 'She done stuck a knife through my hand.'

'Our pa'll hunt you down if you – if you harm us,' she warned.

'That'll be a mite difficult, little lady,' growled Mike

Hampson, 'seeing how we killed him two days ago.' His statement rocked Josie to the core. A hand shot up to her mouth to stifle her startled gasp.

'Let's get on with it,' said Frank Jasper, gritting his teeth in response to the awful pain emanating from his shattered right ankle. Hampson nodded.

'OK,' he agreed. 'Time for some fun. Jake, grab that no-good little brat over there and stake him out while I keep missy here covered.'

Jake Plummer slipped out of his saddle and moved towards the boy who lay spread-eagled on his front in the grass. 'I bet he's gonna squeal like a pig when we skin him,' he said, flipping the youngster over on to his back.

It was the very moment the dazed Hawk McKenzie had been waiting for. As his shoulder blades touched the grass, he opened his eyes, drew his knife and exploded upwards from the ground with all the speed of a striking rattler. Before Plummer could react, the angry youngster thrust the sharp point of his weapon deep into the man's stomach. The renegade fell away backwards with a scream, clutching the gaping wound in his abdomen with both hands.

'Ride, Josie, ride!' yelled Hawk, as he came to his feet.

She instantly kicked her mount into motion, barging past Frank Jasper before he had time to react. When Hawk saw Hampson bringing his rifle to bear on his sister, he hurled his knife at him with all his might. Unfortunately, in the heat of battle, his throw was rushed and his aim inaccurate. The blade went sailing inches past the renegade's head to bury itself deep in the trunk of nearby tree. As his sister's colt disappeared into the trees on the far side of the narrow clearing, Hawk turned on his heels and sprinted for the copse at his back. A bullet removed a piece of bark from a pine tree inches from his head as he zig-zagged his way to safety.

'Get after the girl, Frank!' yelled Hampson as he leapt from his saddle. 'See what you can do for Jake, Ben. I'm gonna run that little redskin to ground, and when I do he'll wish he'd never been born.'

Hawk went ever deeper into the woods. He had heard the renegades bragging about killing his pa. It meant the children could expect no help. All he could do was run and hide. Josie still had her pistol though, and maybe, if she kept on the move, she might be able to circle back to help him. It was a long shot, but he wouldn't give up all the while there was breath in his body.

In truth he had always been out of his depth, but that hadn't prevented him from giving a good account of himself. One dead renegade and two more seriously incapacitated stood as glowing testimony to his skill and courage. His ma had also managed to cripple another. He knew his pa would be proud of his family.

He suddenly found his escape route blocked by a sheer cliff face. As there was no way he could possibly hope to scale it, he turned left along its base, hopping from rock to rock in an attempt to cover his tracks. In his indecent haste to outrun his pursuer he came a cropper on a moss-covered boulder. He cried out in pain as his left ankle twisted violently beneath him. He fell amongst the rocks, grazing both elbows on the way down. Tears welled up in his eyes as he rocked back and forth upon the ground, gripping his rapidly swelling joint in both hands.

It was here that his sister found him. She went down on one knee beside him, putting a hand on his shoulder. 'Are you hurt bad?' she queried.

'Yeah,' he said. 'I think it's bust. How did you find me?'

'By pure luck,' she admitted. 'I decided I'd have more chance of losing them on foot, so I jumped off my pony and then turned him loose. When I heard you cry I ran straight here.'

'Well ain't this a pretty picture?' said Mike Hampson from his position at the base of the cliff. 'You kids have put me to an awful lot of trouble.'

'Go to hell!' snapped Hawk, grimacing with pain, as Frank Jasper limped on to the scene.

'Looks like I got here just in time,' he said, leaning back against a tall pine.

'I could say the same thing.'

All eyes were instantly turned towards the bearded, bloody figure emerging from the woods at Hampson's back. Joy and relief flooded through the children, emotions which were shock and fear appeared on the faces of the two renegades.

'What's up, fellas, you look as if you've seen a

ghost,' said Curtis McKenzie.

'It can't be,' hissed Hampson, taking an involuntary step backwards. 'We killed you, I saw you fall.' McKenzie shook his dirty, blood-smeared head.

'No,' he said, taking one hand off the rifle he held pointed at the renegade's chest to tap the side of his head. 'You merely winged me. It took me a while to come to and pick up your trail, but I always knew I'd find you eventually.'

'I won't miss this time!' roared Hampson, his rifle spitting fire and lead as he dived towards a bush to his right. His hurried shot went high and wide, as did McKenzie's answering fire. The mountain man instinctively charged towards the underbrush where the renegade was desperately trying to reload his weapon. He drew his hunting knife and fell on top of his enemy with an ear-splitting roar.

When Josie saw the other renegade reach for the navy Colt in his belt, she swiftly drew her own pistol. Planting her feet wide apart, she fanned back the hammer, just as her pa had taught her during their hunting trips, and said, 'Don't even think about it!'

'You ain't got the guts, girl,' he sneered, bringing his gun to bear on her.

The pistol bucked wildly in her hands as she pulled the trigger. A look of pure astonishment formed on Frank Jasper's face as he staggered back a pace. As a bright red stain began to spread across his chest, he fell to his knees, coughed twice, then pitched forward and fell lifelessly face-down in the dirt.

McKenzie and Hampson rolled over and over in the brush, grappling to gain the upper hand as they wrestled for possession of the gleaming knife. First one then the other seemed to be getting on top as the children watched in terrified fascination. When Curtis McKenzie finally managed to drive his right knee up into his opponent's rib-cage, the renegade was forced to relinquish his grip on his knife hand. Before he could recover, McKenzie drove the blade deep into his stomach. Hampson grunted loudly and then lay still.

The children ran to their pa's side as he came to his feet to sweep them up in his powerful arms. 'You kids did good,' he said, smiling through his great fatigue. 'I never dared to hope that I'd find you alive after what they did to your ma.'

'There's still two more of them around somewhere,' warned Hawk as his feet returned to the ground.

'Not any more there ain't,' corrected his pa. 'I took care of them first.'

'Can we go home now?' asked Josie, hugging him tight.

'Yeah, I reckon so,' replied McKenzie, 'not that there's much of a home left for us to go back to.'

'We can always rebuild it,' she insisted, as he led the children away.

17

They stood before the simple wooden marker, a family united in grief. McKenzie said a prayer over the grave and then led the children in singing 'Amazing Grace'. When the brief ceremony was over, he led them back towards the burnt-out ruins of the cabin, lost in his own thoughts. He halted just short of what remained of the charred walls and sighed.

'Could be it's time to pull up stakes and head for California,' he said, thrusting his hands deep into his pants pockets.

'You gotta be kiddin' me?' cried Josie, looking aghast. 'Why on earth would we do such a foolish thing?'

'I'm of a mind to make a fresh start,' he said, looking at each of his children in turn. 'Besides, this is no place to bring up a pair of young'uns. You two need schooling and a better future than I can provide you with out here.'

'Hogwash!' exclaimed Josie, putting her hands on

her hips. 'There ain't nothin' we need to learn that you can't teach us. And as you said yourself, this land ain't gonna remain a wilderness forever. There'll be farms and ranches and towns here one day, and when that happens we'll have all the civilized company we need.'

'That's a fact,' he agreed. 'Once the war between the states is over, there'll be a parcel of folks heading west in search of a new life. But that's one of the things that bothers me. Life ain't gonna be the same once people start settling here. It'll also cause trouble with the Utes.'

'That's why we have to stay,' insisted Josie. 'Who else will look out for the Utes when it happens if we don't?'

'Josie's right,' said Hawk. 'We should stay. We have a good life here and when the newcomers arrive, we can teach them the importance of respecting the land and the people who already live upon it.' McKenzie frowned.

'Is that what you both truly want? To stay?' They both nodded. 'Then I reckon we'd better make a start on rebuilding the cabin.'

'Yeah,' said Josie, with a grin, 'but when we build this one, I get my own room.'

'It's a deal,' agreed McKenzie. 'Now let's get to it, we've got a lot of work ahead of us.'